'You know, y... to stop this,' ...

'Stop what?' Lindy ...

'Running away. I don't know what you're frightened of, Lindy, but I'm not going to hurt you.'

She tilted her chin defiantly at him. 'I'm not frightened of anything, Mike Corrigan. Perhaps I'm merely being careful—careful who I choose to be friendly with.'

'Rubbish! There's something holding you back—it's not being careful, it's being inhibited!'

'How dare you? You know nothing about me or why I'm like I am.'

Mike smiled. 'The other week there was something between us—a spark of attraction, something... Call it what you will, but you fancied me, Lindy Jenkins! You've been avoiding me since then and I want to know what I've done wrong.'

She swallowed. Of course she was frightened of involving herself with someone else...perhaps she'd never be able to trust another man again.

Judy Campbell is from Cheshire. As a teenager she spent a great year at high school in Oregon, USA as an exchange student. She has worked in a variety of jobs, including teaching young children, being a secretary and running a small family business. Her husband comes from a medical family and one of their three grown-up children is a GP. Any spare time—when she's not writing romantic fiction—is spent playing golf, especially in the Highlands of Scotland.

A HUSBAND
TO TRUST

BY
JUDY CAMPBELL

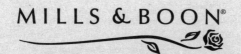

MILLS & BOON®

To Mum, who had the idea, and Donald, my computer expert.

DID YOU PURCHASE THIS BOOK WITHOUT A COVER?

If you did, you should be aware it is **stolen property** as it was reported *unsold and destroyed* by a retailer. Neither the author nor the publisher has received any payment for this book.

All the characters in this book have no existence outside the imagination of the author, and have no relation whatsoever to anyone bearing the same name or names. They are not even distantly inspired by any individual known or unknown to the author, and all the incidents are pure invention.

All Rights Reserved including the right of reproduction in whole or in part in any form. This edition is published by arrangement with Harlequin Enterprises II B.V. The text of this publication or any part thereof may not be reproduced or transmitted in any form or by any means, electronic or mechanical, including photocopying, recording, storage in an information retrieval system, or otherwise, without the written permission of the publisher.

This book is sold subject to the condition that it shall not, by way of trade or otherwise, be lent, resold, hired out or otherwise circulated without the prior consent of the publisher in any form of binding or cover other than that in which it is published and without a similar condition including this condition being imposed on the subsequent purchaser.

MILLS & BOON and MILLS & BOON with the Rose Device are registered trademarks of the publisher.

First published in Great Britain 2001
Harlequin Mills & Boon Limited,
Eton House, 18-24 Paradise Road, Richmond, Surrey TW9 1SR

© Judy Campbell 2001

ISBN 0 263 82671 6

Set in Times Roman 10½ on 12 pt.
03-0601-49794

Printed and bound in Spain
by Litografia Rosés, S.A., Barcelona

PROLOGUE

THE door to the garden was swinging open, the wind sending it crashing backwards and forwards against the wall in the hallway. Michael watched it irritably—he would have liked to have got up and closed it, but Margery had told him to sit down, for heaven's sake, and not to *move* after he'd been such a rowdy boy at lunchtime, teasing all the other boys and making faces at the staff.

Through the glass of the door he could see the little ones skipping round on the grass, and hear them shouting and laughing—any minute they'd be coming in to listen to a story.

There was the sound of giggling and running footsteps. He heard Margery, Oakland Home's Matron, call out in a cross voice, 'Madeline! Madeline! Come back here, you naughty girl, and wait for the others!'

Michael looked up and saw one of the five-year-olds running towards the door, her brown plaits bobbing round her head, her arms outstretched. With a sudden frisson of alarm he noticed that the door was going to slam closed just as she came through. He stood up and shouted, 'Stop! Careful—the door's banging! It'll hit you!'

She didn't hear him. As if in slow motion, he watched the little figure almost float into the door, a thin arm thrusting into the glass, a sudden silence and then a high-pitched wailing from the small body lying on the ground. A jet of blood, like a red fountain, spurted towards Michael, covering the floor and the edge of the curtains by the window.

He stood paralysed for a moment, his heart hammering and his eyes staring in horror at the child's prone figure, the shattered glass lying all over and around her and, most horribly, the increasing amount of blood that was spurting everywhere. He glanced wildly round and then started to shout. The little girl had stopped screaming and was just whimpering softly. Michael's voice sounded strangely squeaky and hoarse.

'Help! Quick, come and help us—there's been an awful accident!'

The blood was still spraying frighteningly out of Madeline's arm, and with a sudden surge of energy Michael forced himself forward and knelt down by her side. She was very pale and he knew he had to do something to stop her losing any more blood. Dimly he remembered seeing a film about a man cutting his leg and a tourniquet being applied. He couldn't remember how you did that, but he pulled a rather grubby handkerchief from his pocket and, folding it like a pad, pressed it to the jagged wound on her arm as hard as he could.

The little girl turned to look at him. She had big dark brown eyes, the colour of beech leaves in autumn, and they were wide with fright.

'It's OK,' gulped Michael, trying to keep his voice calm. 'You'll be fine. It's just a little cut, don't worry. You came like Superwoman through that door!'

He squeezed her hand gently with his free hand.

'I'm not naughty, am I?' she whispered. Then she closed her eyes and her head fell back against Michael's shoulder.

Now there were people filling the room, murmuring

in horror at the sight. Margery ran in from the garden and shooed everyone out, then she crouched down beside the two children, her large presence comforting.

'Eh, Madeline, you poor little lass, what have you done to yourself? Good job Michael was here to help you, wasn't it? By luck, Dr Burford's upstairs, seeing one of the boys, so he'll be here immediately, and he'll soon have you right.'

Dr Burford was tall and lanky with spectacles and a young kind face. He knelt down beside the two children, and gently raised Madeline's arm. She was leaning against Michael, her eyes closed. The doctor turned to the young boy.

'Michael, isn't it? You've done a great job so far. Can you just hold this young lady's arm up high for me while I look at it?'

Michael nodded. He felt a sense of pride that Dr Burford trusted a rowdy ten-year-old to help him. He watched with fascination as the doctor carefully lifted the blood-sodden handkerchief from the wound on Madeline's small arm.

'I think you'll have to throw this away,' he remarked. 'And Madeline will have to have a trip to hospital and get the wound cleaned and stitched—but there's nothing to worry about. She's going to be fine, thanks to your prompt action.'

There was a sudden lightening of the tense atmosphere—somehow, with Dr Burford there, things didn't seem so frightening. Michael watched as the doctor took a dressing pack from his bag, opened it and took out a large gauze pad which he pressed firmly over the wound. The bleeding seemed to have slowed down.

'Did *you* put the hanky on?' he asked Michael.

'Yes... I didn't know what to do, it looked bad. I didn't know how to stop the bleeding.'

Dr Burford smiled at him. 'You couldn't have done anything better—well done! What we've got to do now is keep pressure on the wound and elevate her arm— to try to prevent more blood escaping.'

Michael glowed with pleasure. Usually he was being told off for being boisterous and noisy—he was always getting into trouble. Perhaps for once he'd got it right!

The ambulance had arrived and two men in a green uniform with PARAMEDIC written across a band on their chests came in with a wheelchair.

'How is she, Doctor?' asked one of the men.

Dr Burford looked up. He had a stethoscope in his ears and was listening to Madeline's heart.

'Bit shocked,' he said quietly. 'BP 60/40 and tachycardic. I'd like some blood substitute put in on the way to hospital, and give her some oxygen. I'll follow you in.'

Michael watched Dr Burford with increasing admiration. The doctor was so calm. He knew exactly what to do—he had the whole situation in hand. Madeline's eyes were open now, and she even managed a weak smile as she was borne away, a small pale figure wrapped in a blanket. Dr Burford turned to Michael and patted his shoulder.

'You did a good job there. Most people would have gone to pieces with that sort of shock. You're a natural! You can certainly cope in an emergency!'

And that was when Michael Corrigan, noisy, mischievous cheeky Michael Corrigan, knew that when he grew up he wanted to be a doctor, too.

CHAPTER ONE

THE photo on the bulletin board looked like the publicity shot for an impossibly handsome film star—short spiky haircut, blue eyes crinkled with humour and a full smile showing white even teeth. Underneath the photo, someone had written in startling black letters on a large label, 'You can treat *my* palpitations any time, Doc!'

There was a more sober notice to the side, written in Janet Lessiter's neat handwriting. 'Welcome to Dr Michael Corrigan, our new Casualty SHO. Starting Monday April 3rd.'

Lindy Jenkins squinted at the photo as she wiped the whiteboard clean, and smiled with detached amusement. If this guy wasn't spoken for already, he'd be killed in the rush! He was going to need more than good looks to survive in St Luke's A and E Department, she thought drily—a skin as tough as a rhino's and a thriving sense of humour counted more than the face that launched a thousand films!

'Wow! Where did this gorgeous fella come from?' Sheila Watson, standing at Lindy's elbow, gaped at the photo appreciatively. 'And just think—your horoscope told you this week to step out of the fast lane and grab at new romance!'

Lindy raised one sceptical eyebrow, and pulled off the cheeky text below the photo. '*What* fast lane? The most exciting thing I do at the moment is try a new low-cal fish meal and go to the gym!' Her voice sharpened. 'And if you don't mind, Staff Nurse Watson, we're due to take over in ten minutes, so could we forget about romance for an hour or two?'

She sounded more impatient than she'd intended and she touched Sheila's arm apologetically. 'Sorry, love, didn't mean to snap—bad hair day today—but we'd better check how many sutures and sterile needle packs we have before the fun begins!'

She marched purposefully to one of the treatment rooms and took down some requisition sheets. Sheila looked at her, puzzled. It wasn't like Lindy to be prickly—in the hairiest of moments in A and E she kept her cool. She shrugged—everyone was allowed a blip occasionally. Her stocky little figure trotted behind Lindy and pulled a face.

'You're such a cynic, Lindy. Sometimes these horoscopes predict things really accurately.'

Lindy laughed wryly. 'Perhaps they'll be able to predict how long dear old St Luke's can keep going as a district hospital, then—I'd just like to know that we're going to keep our jobs! Help me swing this trolley round, will you?'

Sheila gave the trolley a hard push so that it swung against the wall and released more space in the small cubicle.

She sighed mournfully. 'If the hospital goes, our jobs go—and before we've got to know this fabulous Dr Corrigan too…' Her voice trailed off dejectedly.

'You man-eater, you!' teased Lindy. She snapped shut a cupboard door and flicked a look at her watch. 'Now let's get this department up and running—and on time! It's eight-thirty a.m. now and one thing I do know for sure—if George Clooney himself was to walk in at this very moment my pulse rate wouldn't go up a notch! As far as I'm concerned, a whole battalion of drop-dead gorgeous men dressed only in running shorts couldn't excite me!'

There was a slight cough behind them and the curtains to the cubicle swished apart. An impressively tall figure dressed in leathers, a large safety helmet and visor seemed to dwarf the entire entrance. The figure made an attempt to pull off the helmet, then gave up.

'Damn thing! Far too small!' said a muffled voice. 'Sorry to butt in, but could you tell me how to find Dr Janet Lessiter? I've been told to see her this morning, but I'm cutting it a bit fine—jammed clutch!'

'Patients—don't you just love 'em?' Lindy growled to herself. On this particular morning she would have appreciated the boost of an uninterrupted brandy more than coffee before they started work—but some patients seemed completely oblivious to the notices spread in gigantic print around the unit— 'Please book into Reception on arrival and wait to be assessed.'

'Dr Lessiter's probably down the corridor and through those double doors.' Lindy said briskly, hiding her irritation from the leather-clad figure. 'I'm afraid you can't just go straight through, even if your GP has sent you. You'll be assessed by the triage nurse, and seen in order of the gravity of your condition. Book into Reception first.'

Lindy waited with some impatience at the slight hiatus whilst the man struggled with his helmet and visor, eventually wrenching them off and holding them under his arm. She did a double-take as the man's head was revealed. Film-star looks all right—a face with a humorous air of suppressed energy, a short and spiky haircut and blue eyes the colour of a tropical sea! She swallowed in surprise as she recognized the Adonis from the photo on the bulletin board.

It was ridiculous, but suddenly she wished she'd made more of an effort with herself that morning, acutely aware that her face hadn't a vestige of make-up—she probably looked like a ghost. And why on earth hadn't she blown her hair dry instead of towelling it roughly into a wild halo after the shower? Mind you, even crawling into her trousers had been an effort that morning. She'd been astonished she'd managed to get to work at all, today of all days.

The photo didn't do the man justice—it didn't convey the air of confidence and self-possession he exuded. He was the kind of guy who made you wish you'd stuck more rigorously to a fat-free diet for longer than one day, Lindy thought ruefully. And she'd bet her bottom dollar that he was well aware of the impression he made. Furthermore, she was sure that he'd heard her remarks about men and was having a good laugh at her expense!

The man swept an appraising glance over Lindy's tall and well-proportioned figure, noting the challenging spark in her large dark eyes and the 'I'm in charge' message they sent out.

'Ah!' He leaned back casually against a cupboard, and explained smilingly, 'There was no one in Reception a minute ago. I'm not actually a patient—it's as a colleague that I need to meet Dr Lessiter. I'm the new SHO in Casualty.'

Lindy and Sheila exchanged quick glances—did the poor fellow know what he was letting himself in for? The last SHO had left after a terrible dust-up with Janet Lessiter, the specialist registrar in A and E and the most irritable woman in the hospital. Years of being overworked and understaffed seemed to have turned her into a woman most people would rather avoid. Would this guy be up to the job? From the way he was propping himself against the supplies cupboard, he seemed totally relaxed—a very good quality when dealing with Janet!

Lindy pulled a wry face. 'Sorry about that. We knew you were coming today—there's a photo of you on the bulletin board, but you were hard to recognise behind the visor! We get so many people trying to jump the queue that we've got to be really firm. It's nice to meet you—I'm Lindy Jenkins, and this is Sheila Watson.'

He squinted at her name badge. 'Sister Lindy Jenkins, Emergency Nurse Practitioner—you'll know more than me, I expect.'

She smiled. 'I doubt it. We've done this all-singing, all dancing-course, and now we can do more procedures than we used to. It's supposed to save time, but I think we just get more people in to fill the slack!'

'There's always too many patients!' The man held out a strong hand and shook theirs. 'I'm Mike Corrigan—no doubt we'll be seeing plenty of each other.'

He smiled a slow, charismatic smile at them both, and Sheila blushed to the roots of her hair, bolting out of the cubicle to answer the phone when it rang in the main corridor.

Mike Corrigan looked down at Lindy with a twinkle in the blue eyes and an impish smile touching his lips. 'I don't know if George Clooney *is* waiting in Reception, but it looks as if you're in for a busy day—plenty of customers there!'

So he *had* overheard her remarks regarding men! Lindy coloured slightly. She must have sounded ever so slightly paranoid! She tried to think of something reasonably normal to say.

'Have you worked in this area before?' she asked brightly.

'I was brought up here and trained at the old Infirmary—but I don't think we've ever worked together before, have we?'

He looked at her rather lingeringly, and not for the first time Lindy wished her uniform of tunic and trousers was slightly snappier and not quite so figure-hugging. He frowned thoughtfully, a faintly puzzled look on his face.

'It's a funny thing, though—I do feel I've met you somewhere before. Ridiculous really—surely I wouldn't have forgotten working with an attractive woman like you!' He grinned, his eyes locking with hers for a second.

A flash of irritation darted through Lindy—she might have known a good-looking male would flirt with anyone who had a heartbeat and was female! This Mike Corrigan was no different after all to any other confident guy who expected women to respond to his crass chat-up lines.

She wasn't going to be taken in by that sort of thing again. She'd really had enough of sexy-looking men with nothing behind the façade—men who thought they were God's gift to women! And today of all days, she reflected bitterly, should be a reminder of that lesson. Still, for purely professional reasons she'd like to know more about him.

'Where was your last job?' she asked brusquely.

'I was struggling to keep pace in a casualty unit in inner city New York—fairly hairy, but I loved it. Could have stayed there for a long time, but things happen to change one's plans, and now I find I'm back where I started.'

Despite herself, Lindy was impressed. Working in an inner city A and E in somewhere like New York certainly wasn't a soft option.

'So what made you come back to a town like Manorfield? After the Big Apple it must seem a bit of a backwater,' she asked curiously.

Something happened to his expression. A bleak shadow crossed his face, and his mouth tightened briefly.

'Things happened at home—I felt I was needed here.'

Lindy bit her lip. She'd obviously put her big fat foot in it somewhere and touched a raw nerve. Mr Confident wasn't as bright and breezy as he made out! It was no big deal—she had quite a respect for people who didn't blab about their private lives. After all, she had her own reasons for holding on to her private space.

He shrugged slightly, as if pushing away negative thoughts, and smiled engagingly.

'I'll be able to visit my old haunts and perhaps find some new ones. Are you a local girl?'

'Afraid so—lived here all my life.'

'Ah—then I shall rely on you to show me what Manorfield has to offer these days.'

His laughing eyes caught hers, holding them a fraction too long. They were a clear cobalt blue that seemed to look right into her soul, and for a second Lindy forgot she was in St Luke's Casualty on day shift. Suddenly she felt a ripple of…what? Excitement? Irritation? Surely not *attraction*?

She swallowed in annoyance. She couldn't believe

she was feeling these emotions so soon after Jake, responding like a gawky teenager and buckling at the knees at the sight of an attractive man like Mike Corrigan. After the experience she'd had, Lindy had been sure that it would be a long, long time before she responded to any man, let alone this stranger.

She looked at him warily, uneasily conscious of his appealing aura and irritated both by his assumption that she was only too willing and available to jump to his bidding and at her own unprofessional response to him.

'I'm sure you'll be able to find your own way about,' she said coolly. 'It's not changed much over the years.'

'Perhaps not.' He looked at her thoughtfully for a second as if he'd caught her negative vibes, then picked up a battered bag at his feet and threw his helmet and visor inside, slinging it easily over his shoulder.

'Be seeing you, Sister Jenkins. By the way,' he added with a grin, as he paused at the curtains of the cubicle, 'if we should take a break through the morning, I'm very fond of black coffee with three spoonfuls of sugar when you put on the kettle!'

'What a cheek,' muttered Lindy, torn, despite herself, between amusement and aggravation at his presumption as she watched his tall figure disappear down the corridor.

Then she gave an unwilling giggle as she wondered what Janet Lessiter, without much of a sense of humour, would make of his relaxed, jokey manner. Maybe, just maybe, he might be the one to weather the storms!

Sheila bustled back in with eyes as big as saucers. 'Wow! Is that Michael Corrigan gorgeous or isn't he?' she demanded. 'Those eyes and that smile! Don't tell me you didn't notice them, Lindy Jenkins!'

'I certainly did not!' Lindy's voice was sharp.

'I love blue eyes in a man,' reflected Sheila dreamily.

'I never noticed,' said Lindy tartly.

Sheila gave a hoot of laughter. 'I don't believe you.' She added slyly, 'That man would make anyone weak at the knees!'

Lindy scowled and threw a ball of paper at her. 'Apart from the fact that the man's probably married with three children, he won't last long here, will he? Not with Janet Lessiter as a boss! None of the SHOs stay very long in this department—in fact, who'd want a permanent job here if they thought the place was closing down?'

Sheila shrugged. 'If you ask me, one casualty unit's much like another, and Mike Corrigan looks the type that can handle anything—even one of Janet's tantrums! If her reputation's gone before her, he probably looks on it as a challenge. And anyway,' she said stoutly, 'Manorfield's a great place to live—full of history, lots of nightlife and right near the countryside. Who wouldn't be happy living here?'

Simple, isn't it? reflected Lindy wryly, chalking up the names of patients on the large whiteboard. Live in a nice place, eat plenty of comfort food, buy lots of new clothes and you should be perfectly happy. Only it didn't always work like that...

Mike smiled to himself as he strode through the wide main corridor of A and E. Despite everything, things were looking up! There was a streak of optimism in his nature that flared into life fairly easily. A beautiful girl in his department was enough to brighten his day considerably, and cancel out the negative thoughts he'd been having about this new job and that ogress, Janet Lessiter, who was his new boss.

Lindy Jenkins was a knockout, he mused appreciatively, with her statuesque figure and slightly wild bob of glossy dark hair. There was something about her that fascinated him. He was getting a message that definitely said, Keep your distance. And yet there was a fire of challenge which he could read in her eyes. And here a chord of memory seemed to vibrate in his mind. Those dark tawny eyes—the colour of beech leaves in autumn—reminded him of someone he'd once met, though who or when he couldn't remember.

Mike laughed at himself, wondering where he'd picked that fanciful phrase about her eyes from. Weren't they just ordinary tawny irises with flecks of gold in them, surrounded, as he remembered, with a fan of long lashes curving against her cheek when she looked down? He would, he thought jauntily, get to know her better—as Sheila had guessed, Michael Corrigan liked a challenge. Not that he was thinking of romance. He had too much on his plate at the moment, with family affairs and a new job, for any sort of relationship, and anyway a girl like her was bound to have a partner in the background. Still…a picture of those dark eyes and the defensive light in them swam before him pleasurably for a moment.

His expression hardened. Funny how life had a way of turning full circle and now he was back where he'd started out. He sighed. Difficult bosses were the least of his problems—his main concern now had to be five-year-old Max. Looking after a wilful little boy was going to be hellish difficult, but Max was the reason Mike had come back to Manorfield.

The child had been through so much, and no way

would he abandon the little boy to a repetition of his own childhood.

The unit was really humming now. A barrage of people swirled round the reception area, and the constant swishing of the automatic doors admitted yet more patients. Although A and E stayed open all night, there was always a build-up of non-urgent cases at the start of the day, whilst emergencies from the night before were still being dealt with. They had already dealt with an old lady's fractured hip, an overdose and a bad cycling accident.

Lindy, Sheila and Carrie Brennan, a student nurse, were gathered round the big whiteboard where Lindy was filling in the squares with a list of patients in the various cubicles and résumés of their afflictions. In the emergency rooms behind them Janet battled to get the hip fracture a bed on a ward and Mike and the rest of the team dealt with the result of the accident.

'Right! Let's get going on this list,' said Lindy briskly. 'Cubicle one—elderly lady, Mrs Janus, fell in the high street and has a badly cut knee. Carrie, go and clean it up, ask if she's had a tetanus injection, take a detailed history, BP, etc., and make sure she hasn't injured anything else. If you're worried, ask! Sheila, you take Mr Morland in two. He caught his finger in the car door—he'll need an X-ray. I'll deal with this six-year-old, Miranda Fyles-Smith, in cubicle three.'

Carrie had caught sight of Mike Corrigan's photo on the bulletin board, and gave a low whistle.

'Now, when did he arrive?' she asked in her soft Irish lilt. 'I bet *he's* got a lovely bedside manner! Do you think it's just possible he's free and needing a

young girl to show him around? Because I'm only too
willing to help!'

'Very possibly,' observed Lindy rather tartly as she
swept into cubicle three. Crossly she hoped all the female staff weren't going to lose their marbles over this
man. Sheila and Carrie seemed too easily distracted by
any males who weren't actually in a coma! Mike
Corrigan wasn't a pin-up—he was here to do a job of
work, and so were they!

It wasn't Miranda Fyles-Smith's fault that she had such
an obnoxious mother, Lindy reflected wearily, but it
certainly made dealing with the child very difficult!
Mrs Fyles-Smith was wearing impeccably cut black
trousers and a beautiful camel-hair jacket. Streaked
blond hair was held back by two tortoiseshell clips, and
perfect make-up made the best of a rather horsy-
looking face.

'This is just too awful,' she whined in a nasal voice.
'We've been waiting simply hours. I really don't know
how anyone puts up with this dreadful service. I'm due
out at lunch fairly soon, and the wretched au pair is in
bed with some lurgy or other and couldn't bring
Miranda herself... Could you make it snappy, please?'

Lindy, reflecting on the whirlwind morning she'd already had, smiled pleasantly, from long practice managing to hide her real thoughts.

'We have seen Miranda as soon as possible. She's
already had her X-ray, which shows she's got a simple
fracture of the radius bone—just a little crack. All we
need to do is immobilise it by plastering it, and it'll be
as good as new in a few weeks.'

Miranda, a plump child with red hair, round owlish

glasses and wearing an unbecoming school uniform, burst into tears.

'Oh, God, what a bore. Do pull yourself together, darling. Perhaps it'll teach you not to be so clumsy.' The mother tapped impatient fingers on her handbag.

Miranda's sobs doubled and Lindy bent down and smiled reassuringly at her, putting an arm round her plump shoulders. The child was frightened, and she wasn't getting too much tender loving care from her mother! Lindy gently took hold of Miranda's arm and pointed to the concave 'dish' of the fracture.

'That's where the crack is—when the plaster's on, it won't hurt at all. Now, tell me how you hurt yourself, love—did you fall in the playground? I want to know all about it.'

As a ploy to distract Miranda it was fairly successful. The young girl snivelled and rubbed her eyes with her knuckles, pushing aside her glasses and trying to concentrate on her story.

She whispered, 'I was coming down the slide on my knees and I...I fell over the edge, onto Jane Gosforth. It really hurt.'

'One can only say, "Poor Jane Gosforth!" I shouldn't think she's feeling too good after you've fallen on her!' Mrs Fyles-Smith sat carefully on a chair and crossed elegant legs.

Lindy saw the stricken expression on Miranda's face and tried to minimise her mother's wounding words by smiling kindly at the child and giving her a wink. 'It's much more exciting coming down a slide that way, isn't it? I expect you quite like doing daring things, don't you?'

Miranda blinked—she'd obviously never thought of herself as daring or brave. She smiled a watery smile at Lindy, who gently pulled a tube of heavy gauze over the injured arm. Miranda winced and stared nervously at her thumb as it was pulled through the small loop Lindy had made in the gauze.

'That's as bad as it gets,' soothed Lindy. 'All we've got to do is wind this plaster bandage round your arm, and that won't take long. Keep as still as possible.'

Miranda gulped and hiccoughed, and suddenly Lindy felt intensely sorry for the little girl. What must it be like to have a mother like hers, solely concerned with her own life? The child was trying her best to be brave.

'That's great—you're being very helpful, Miranda,' murmured Lindy as she supported the elbow on a padded block of wood and carefully wound the plaster-impregnated bandage round the child's arm. 'When I've finished, you'll be able to get everyone to autograph your plaster.'

Mrs Fyles-Smith yawned and drew out a mobile phone from her handbag.

Lindy looked up quickly. 'I'm sorry, Mrs Fyles-Smith, you'll have to switch off your mobile—they can upset equipment in the hospital.'

'Oh, for heaven's sake—this is the last straw. I really don't feel like being told what to do by nursing staff. It's imperative I call my luncheon date and tell him I'm going to be late—I'm sorry!' Long red fingernails started to tap out numbers on the mobile.

Lindy's blood began to boil. 'If you wish to use your mobile you must go outside—you could be putting patients' lives at risk.'

Mrs Fyles-Smith rose from her chair. 'Don't be so ridiculously melodramatic,' she snapped. 'Come on, darling, she looks as if she's finished with you now...'

'Remember to come back tomorrow morning to the fracture clinic and have the plaster checked.' Lindy didn't know if the woman had heard her, for she swept out of the cubicle without a backwards glance, Miranda stumping along behind her rather dejectedly.

Lindy quickly tidied up the cubicle and took the bowl of plaster to the basins outside the cubicle, still seething with fury. Mrs Fyles-Smith hadn't moved far—she was standing by the desks, which had an array of computer equipment on them, and continuing an animated conversation on her mobile.

How satisfying it would be to chuck the whole bowl of liquid plaster over the woman! Lindy started to stride across the floor, her cheeks flushed and a steely glint in her eye. Surely she could plead mitigating circumstances if she did set the woman in plaster—after all, today she did have an excuse for being on a short fuse!

A restraining hand caught her arm, and a voice murmured, 'I know how you feel, but shall I intervene before you murder Mrs Vile Smith?'

Lindy chuckled—a fairly apt nickname! Mike Corrigan's tall figure had risen from behind one of the computers he'd been working at, and he gave her a wink before strolling over to the woman and taking the mobile firmly out of her hand.

'I don't think so,' he said quietly.

'Do you mind? This is a private conversation!'

'Not here it's not,' said Mike pleasantly, but firmly.

Mrs Fyles-Smith whipped round, her eyes blazing with fury, her expression changing somewhat as she took in Mike Corrigan's impressive height and heady looks. He spoke loudly and clearly to her.

'Perhaps you didn't hear Sister Jenkins the first time.

Nobody is allowed to use mobiles in the hospital—they can jam up life-saving equipment.' Mike switched off the phone before handing it back to her.

Lindy held her breath. How would that ghastly woman react to being told off again?

Mrs Fyles-Smith after her initial shock, gave a brilliant smile and, looking at him coquettishly, said in a throaty voice, 'I *do* apologise, Doctor—er, Dr Corrigan, is it? How thoughtless of me! I really had no idea.... Bringing my daughter in for this awful emergency has made me feel terribly flustered and rather late for an appointment...'

Mike nodded politely and walked briskly back to the treatment rooms without waiting to hear the end of the woman's excuse. Lindy almost cheered to see Mrs Fyles-Smith's rather crestfallen look—he obviously had the measure of the woman!

Chuckling, she wiped Miranda's name from the whiteboard. In his own way Mike Corrigan was just as tough as Janet Lessiter but with added charm. She was impressed at the neat way he'd dealt with the situation.

She pulled out the next card and entered the patient's name where Miranda's had been on the board, then walked to the waiting room. The usual group of bored or restless people lounged on the rows of chairs. A child was crying and a group of youths was laughing and shouting loudly at each other. They were grouped under the enormous wall-mounted television which seemed to be on day and night, a perpetual background murmur to the noise going on in front of it from the waiting patients. She went over to Jenny Forest, the receptionist.

'Keep an eye on those lads, Jenny. Any trouble, call the porter!'

She turned back to the waiting room. 'Albert Simpson, please!'

An elderly stout man shuffled forward, holding a handkerchief to his eye.

'I'm in agony, Nurse,' he said hoarsely. 'I was chopping up wood, and it feels like I've got a huge branch in my eye! I felt it fly in like a bullet.'

'Come into this cubicle,' said Lindy with a smile. 'I'm sure I can make it more comfortable for you. Just sit on the chair and I'll look at it through the ophthalmoscope. If I can't deal with it, we'll get the ophthalmic surgeon to look at it.'

It was easy enough to see the offending particle, and it took only a matter of seconds to roll back the lid of Mr Simpson's eye and irrigate it, removing the microscopic splinter that had been causing him such pain. She showed him the particle on a piece of tissue, and gently swabbed his eye with a mild antiseptic solution.

'I don't see any scratch marks—you've been lucky. But, for heaven's sake, wear some protective goggles next time!'

Mr Simpson blinked gingerly and then grinned. 'Thanks, Nurse. It's a miracle—I thought my eye was coming out!'

A sudden commotion in the large area beyond the cubicle made them both jump. Sounds of a scuffle and various oaths floated through the curtains. Mr Simpson met Lindy's eyes with alarmed interest.

'What in tarnation's happening? Sounds like a blooming revolution's taking place.'

'Wait here for a moment, Mr Simpson,' said Lindy grimly. 'I'll just go and find out.'

It wasn't unusual for some sort of fracas to develop

at some time between patients, or even between patients and staff—but not often on a Monday morning!

Two wild-eyed youths with shaven heads and wearing grubby white vests were locked together in a frenzy of flailing limbs and kicking boots in the square of space near the desks. Blood was dripping copiously over the floor, and two or three teenagers had pushed forward from the waiting area and were cheering the assailants on.

'Hell,' Lindy swore between her teeth. She looked round quickly for Jack Hulse, the rather slow porter. At least he was large and strong and had broken up a few fights in the past. No sign of him. She slammed the alarm bell with her hand and marched over to the yelling youths watching the performance. From the corner of her eye she could see alarmed and fascinated faces peering at the scene from the waiting room.

'Go and sit down,' she shouted above the noise. 'You won't be seen at all unless you return to your seats.'

She stood in front of them with her arms folded, looking as impassive as possible. She usually found that looking as if you weren't at all fazed by any aggression seemed to calm things down. They stared back at her blankly. Then reluctantly, calling out what they thought were witticisms, they strolled back to their seats.

Sheila appeared from a cubicle and looked with raised eyebrows at the duo still slugging it out in a grunting kind of brawl in front of her.

'Here we go again. Shall we have a go at separating them?' It was getting to be such a regular occurrence that she hardly looked surprised.

Lindy shook her head. 'Let them get rid of a bit of

energy for a few minutes. Security should be here soon.'

Suddenly one of the boys wriggled free and pushed his opponent to the ground, kicking the other boy's head savagely with his huge black boots. The air was filled with screams and oaths and, on auto-response, Lindy leapt forward and grabbed the youth's collar from the back, hanging on like a terrier with a bone.

'No, you don't!' she yelled ineffectually. The youth tried to shake her off irritably, as one would a wasp, and one of the rings on his flailing hands caught her arm, scraping it like a bread knife so that a red weal appeared on the skin. Lindy staggered back and fell against the wall, cursing herself that she'd allowed him to get her off balance.

A voice as hard as steel unexpectedly cut through the noise.

'What the hell's going on?'

A tall figure appeared from nowhere, grabbing the boy's arms and pinning them fiercely behind his back, forcing the youth to the floor on his stomach. Michael Corrigan flung himself on the lad's wriggling, squirming body, and straddled him with powerful legs.

'Proud of yourself, are you? Managed to knock a nurse down—what a big man! Perhaps someone could pass me some masking tape and I'll make this gentleman more secure.'

'Let me go, you bastard,' yelled the youth. 'I'll have you up for assault!'

'I've only been very gentle with you so far, mate,' retorted Mike, deftly binding the man's wrists. 'Wait till I get really angry…'

Lindy blew her cheeks out in relief, her heart hammering with exertion and fright. Thank God Mike had appeared before the minor skirmish had become a major one. There were too many of these fights happening, and it was taking too long for Security to materialise. She glanced up at the CCTV camera and hoped to goodness that there was a film in it—it would be important evidence when the men were prosecuted for causing an affray.

'Pity they didn't knock each other out,' Mike remarked, standing up and dusting off his white coat. 'Where's all the blood coming from? Are they patients?'

Sheila bent down and inspected the boy who was moaning.

'Nothing life-threatening…'

'Pity.' Mike grinned.

'One of his earrings has split his lobe,' she reported. 'That's what's making the mess. I'll have to clean it up now. And apparently they're just mates of someone waiting in Casualty—rival gangs, it seems, still pretty topped up with the weekend's booze if you ask me.'

'Sounds just like New York,' observed Mike.

Two security men burst in and the youths were quickly hauled to their feet, handcuffed and led unwillingly to an interview room to wait for the police to come.

Mike bent down towards Lindy, who was still sitting against the wall and rubbing her elbow.

'Are you OK? Hurt your back?'

She shook her head. 'Nope—just my dignity. I was only trying to stop him braining his friend.'

'No chance of that,' Mike chuckled. 'There isn't a brain cell between them. You should have left them to it—let them slug it out together rather than compromise

your own safety. Why should you risk hurting yourself
to save their ugly mugs?'

He smiled down at her, then, as she began to struggle
up, he slipped his arms under hers and pulled her up
as easily as if she were a small child rather than a
statuesque five feet eight inches!

She gave a gasp of surprise as she felt the strength
in his arms, and her heart beat a nervous tattoo against
her chest. She had a fleeting suggestion of how it might
feel to be held against this man's powerful chest with
his arms around her, and it felt good—too darned good!
A cold shiver ran through her. She didn't want to think
of being held in a man's arms today—she felt too vul-
nerable, too lacerated by recent events to need that kind
of bitter-sweet reminder.

She pulled away from him quickly, her voice defensive. 'I'm fine, thanks. Just going to put something on
this scratch.'

A trickle of blood had oozed from her arm and drib-
bled onto Mike's white coat. He took her arm gently
and turned it to see the cut. Next to the fresh wound
was an old scar, jagged and white, running from the
crease in her elbow to the wrist.

'Looks as if this arm has already had some punish-
ment,' he observed drily. 'Don't tell me you make a
habit of separating thugs... You must have had a bad
accident some time.' He frowned as if recalling something.

Lindy snatched her arm away sharply. That scar was
another thing from her past, another life, and it didn't
concern anyone else, least of all Mike Corrigan, whom
she'd only just met. The more someone knew about
you, the more power they had over you.

'It happened a long time ago when I was a child,'

she said curtly. 'If you don't mind, I'll just go and swab the cut.'

She turned on her heel and walked briskly away, her stomach churning. She'd known today would be difficult—Mike Corrigan's arrival seemed to have made it more so and for some reason disturbed her already shaky equilibrium.

Of course, she reflected sadly, he wasn't to know that today should have been her wedding day. She checked her watch. At this precise moment she should have been walking down the aisle.

CHAPTER TWO

JANET LESSITER stared angrily at the circle of doctors and nurses standing round the bulletin board, her stout, short body threatening to burst out of the hospital greens she was wearing.

'I have just been told by Human Resources,' she said, managing to invest those words with the deepest scorn, 'that there will be no agency nurses available for the next few days, even though we have three staff off with flu. I'm afraid it will be turmoil here for a while, but we'll just have to do the best we can.'

She turned to glare at Ray Hunter, a casualty officer who was whispering something to Staff Nurse Verity Marshall. He was a small, mild man who seemed perpetually anxious and jumped nervously when she spoke to him in her usual terse manner.

'Ray and Sister Jenkins, work out a new rota as quickly as possible between you—some of us may have to do double shifts. I should be obliged if coffee-breaks could be kept to a minimum, and that we keep good timing…'

Her abrupt voice trailed off as the doors thumped open and all eyes turned to a familiar dark-haired leather-clad figure striding towards them, blue eyes twinkling. Without warning, Lindy felt her cardiac rate bound unaccountably into overdrive, as it had all week whenever Mike appeared. She was baffled and annoyed by her reaction to the man. In so many ways he had the kind of confidence, bordering almost on boldness,

31

that she had learned to despise. Didn't it go hand in hand with a selfish disregard for other people's feelings?

Nevertheless she ruefully conceded that her resolution to regard Mike from a strictly professional standpoint seemed to be going down the tube! It was odd how she missed him if he wasn't there, and was intensely aware of him when he was—and she wasn't the only one, she reflected, looking at Sheila, Carrie and Verity, all standing up straighter and pulling their bottoms and stomachs in! She shrugged her shoulders. She supposed her reaction was merely because she'd got used to the other, more ordinary male members of staff—Mike did rather stand out beside them!

He propped himself nonchalantly on a desk edge. His body, encased tightly in his biker's gear, looked lean and powerful—and frankly raunchy!

Janet glowered at him and looked pointedly at her watch. 'I was just saying, Dr Corrigan, that I would appreciate strict time-keeping if you don't mind— we're several staff short.'

He glanced round with a cheery grin. 'Sorry, folks, minute or two behind time. Fuel injection's thrombosed—couldn't get the thing to start!' He rubbed his hands together. 'Ready for action now!'

Lindy couldn't help giggling at the nonplussed expression on Janet's face. Most people would have prostrated themselves on the floor before her, but Mike's manner was full of charm and humour. Surely not even Janet could take offence for long!

The standby phone rang suddenly and shrilly by Lindy's arm, preventing Janet from blowing her top completely. It was the 999 call most of them dreaded, for it could mean anything from a multiple road traffic accident to a very sick child. Everyone was silent and stiffened slightly, preparing for action as Lindy answered it.

'St Luke's A and E—Lindy Jenkins here.' She listened intently for a second. 'Right, I have that. Badly injured male, chest crushed by falling debris on a building site, very low BP, status 3, and three other males with minor injuries—lacerations and bruising, possible arm fracture. ETA about seven minutes.'

She looked up at Janet who nodded, her staccato voice briskly rapping out the action plan. 'We're ready. Mike, change out of that ridiculous outfit, and you and Lindy gown up and take the chest case. Ray, Verity and I will deal with the other three. Sounds as if we'd better get Mr Gordon and his team on standby if the status 3 needs surgery. Sheila, check the emergency room. Can we free any cubicles yet?'

Suddenly there was the bustle of controlled chaos as equipment, trolleys and people were moved to await the influx of patients. Before long, the faint sound of the ambulance siren could be heard coming up the drive, whining down to silence as it parked by the doors to Casualty. The doors swished open and the first emergency was pushed in at a trot.

Lindy ran beside the paramedics, one of them holding up a drip from the man on the trolley. 'Name's Alfred Talbot. Age 40, BP dropping rapidly, 85/40, pulse rapid, 125. Got an airway in, but it's not doing much good...' panted one of them.

Alfred Talbot was pushed into the emergency room, and Mike bent over the patient's large, inert body. The man had an enormous stomach over which was stretched a T-shirt and jeans. He made no sound, but his face was deathly pale and he shook as if he had a rigor. Lindy quickly cut away his shirt and the fastening of his jeans, and Mike sounded out his chest with his stethoscope. Sheila had put a Dynamap on his arm which indicated his blood pressure every few seconds, and a mask was slipped over his face to deliver oxygen to his labouring body.

'Bloods and cross-match—we need at least six units,' Mike said tersely. 'He's haemorrhaging badly—could be he's ruptured his liver or lungs. Get some Haemaccel into him fast, while I find out what's happening. What's his BP?'

'Low—systolic's dropped from 85 to 70, and diastolic's 40.'

'Get that infusion going in quickly and use the blood-warmer—he's cyanosed.'

Lindy set up the drip and glanced at the patient's blue lips and cheeks. His heart and lungs were in stress, and they needed to counter the decline in blood he was losing.

'Increasing rate of infuser,' she murmured.

Mike's hands moved carefully over the man's abdomen, his strong fingers palpating gently but firmly around the man's ribcage and sternum, feeling for signs of bleeding from vital organs. He stared in concentration at a spot on the wall in front of him as his hands searched for clues to the problem, then suddenly he lifted his head and looked up with a faint triumphant smile.

'Bingo! Looks like a traumatic pneumothorax—we'll have to put a tap in the chest and get him stable until the theatre team are ready to operate on the other damage he's done to himself. I guess this guy's fractured a rib and torn a lung.'

Lindy and Sheila flicked a glance at each other.

Alfred Talbot was dangerously near death. The leakage of air and blood collecting in the chest cavity meant the heart was under pressure, the lung being prevented from expanding with each inhaled breath.

'Swab his chest please, Nurse, and I'll get some lignocaine into him,' said Mike, pulling on latex gloves.

Lindy pulled the emergency trolley forward, and Sheila surrounded the swabbed area of the man's lower chest with sterile towels. They waited while the local anaesthetic took effect, Lindy watching the man's blood pressure being constantly monitored on the dial.

'OK, Sister—a sharp scalpel, please.' With his left index finger Mike traced the line he needed to cut. Then he made a one-inch incision deep into the chest wall.

'Chest drain, and keep swabbing that blood away.'

Mike plugged the opening of the chest with his finger until the tube was handed to him, then pushed it firmly into the incision, clamped in the middle by a pair of forceps and ending in a bottle half-filled with sterile water. He anchored the drain with two or three stitches.

'Hold your breath, girls,' he muttered. 'Let's see if we get a result…'

He unclipped the forceps from the tube. With a hiss the trapped air in the chest cavity escaped, and blood gushed into the bottle.

Mike blew out his cheeks. 'We have lift-off! Well done, Mr Talbot—now, let's see some colour in your face.' He turned to Lindy, monitoring the machines. 'What's his BP now?'

'Better—100 over 60.'

Mike pulled off his gloves. 'I think he's OK to go to Theatre, then.'

'How's it going—any trouble?' Janet came into the room and looked at Mr Talbot, now breathing with more rhythm. 'Mr Gordon's on his way down. Was it a pneumothorax?'

Mike nodded. 'He's contained now, but still losing blood from somewhere, which the surgeon will sort out. I reckon Mr Talbot's lucky he was a tad over-weight—probably helped to protect his abdomen when he got in the way of that falling debris.' He looked up with a grin at the three women in the room. 'Don't ever go on a diet—could save your life, having a bit of flesh on you!'

'Ah,' said Janet gruffly. 'Then I should be OK!'

Her bleeper started up and she went out of the room. Lindy and Sheila looked at each other with astonish-ment—had Janet Lessiter actually made fun of herself?

Mike stretched his tall frame and rubbed the small of his back cautiously, trying to alleviate the stiffness which had settled there after bending over a patient for twenty minutes.

'Wow, I need caffeine intravenously,' he moaned. 'Is the kettle on?'

Lindy flashed a quick look at him—she was im-pressed. Mike was no mean operator, swift, neat and calm—a complete contrast to Ray Hunter, who, al-though meticulous, worried and fussed about every-thing, which communicated itself to everyone else around him. From the moment he'd examined Alfred Talbot, Lindy had sensed Mike's confidence and abil-ity. He deserved his coffee.

Mike started writing up the patient's notes while Lindy and Sheila gathered up the unsterile towels and threw them in the laundry basket.

'Nice work,' he said quietly. Sheila glowed happily and almost skipped out of the room.

Mike made to follow her, then stopped by Lindy's side, touching her arm. He was close to her—unnervingly close. As a colleague that shouldn't matter at all, except for the fact that his blue eyes held hers in an intimate look which seemed to lock them together in a private and confidential moment. His mouth was only a breath away and, to her astonishment, the crazy thought flashed into her mind as to what his lips would feel like, pressed against hers.

Lightly he brushed some strands of hair from her forehead, his fingers sliding feather-like down her jawline. 'Good going there—we made a great team, didn't we?'

'What?' Lindy dragged her eyes away from that seductive mouth, feeling as if an electric shock had crackled across his face as he'd touched her. 'Yes, sure,' she said hurriedly. 'It went well.'

She turned quickly away to adjust the height of the drip, and wildly wondered what madness was happening with her responses to this man! She had been a fool before, allowed herself to be seduced by charm and good looks—gullible to the point of folly, allowing herself to believe that Jake was an honourable man. Had she learned nothing? Angrily she snapped a clip down on the drip and put the patient's notes on the shelf. She could only ascribe her extraordinary reaction to Mike to the emotional shock she'd had so recently over Jake.

Carrie popped her head round the door. 'Mr Talbot's wife is waiting outside. She's a bit anxious and would like to speak to you. Can she see her husband yet?'

Mike looked across at Lindy and she nodded her head. 'Just let me do a quick tidy-up in here.'

She bent over the patient with relief, breathing deeply and thanking God she could get back to work and forget what Mike's presence was doing to her. Mr Talbot's eyes had fluttered open and he was looking blankly around him over the oxygen mask.

'You're OK, Mr Talbot. You're in Casualty, waiting for an operation to tidy your chest up after an accident you had at work.'

The patient mumbled something unintelligible, and Lindy squeezed his hand. 'Don't worry. Your wife would like to see you for a minute. She's right here.'

Mike came in with a small, frightened-looking woman clutching a large handbag. She looked speechlessly at her husband with the drip, mask and drain attached to him, then pressed a handkerchief to her mouth.

Mike's arm was on her shoulder, and he smiled down at her reassuringly. 'It looks more frightening than it is,' he said gently. 'Your husband's had to have some blood that collected in his chest pumped out before he can have his operation. He's stable now and just waiting for the surgeon.'

Mrs Talbot gulped and nodded and took a tentative step towards her husband, putting a hand gingerly on his arm. 'Alf...you'll be all right, Alf. I don't know what you'll do to yourself next, I really don't...' Her voice faltered and she looked helplessly round at Mike and Lindy. 'He...he's very still, isn't he?'

Lindy patted her arm. It was frightening seeing someone hooked up to all the paraphernalia in the emergency room. Coupled with the shock of hearing about the accident itself, it could make one feel physically ill.

'He's had a bad accident. But it could have been much worse, so try not to worry too much. Why don't I get you a cup of tea while he goes to surgery? You'll feel better after that.'

Mrs Talbot took a last bewildered look at her husband and allowed herself to be led away, Lindy's arm around her shoulder.

Mike looked up quizzically over his cup of coffee as Lindy came into the little kitchen. 'Did you calm Mrs Talbot down?'

She nodded. 'Poor little thing. She said she'd only just come from this hospital, visiting her father who's had his hip done, and then the police came round to her house to tell her about her husband!'

Mike chuckled. 'That's a bit hard—but at least she can do all her visiting at once now! It was a near thing, though,' he reflected. 'Another few minutes and she might not have needed to visit her husband at all...'

There was silence for a few seconds as Lindy poured herself a cup of coffee. Mike sprawled in a chair, his long legs in front of him, watching her reflectively.

'And what made you go into nursing?' he asked suddenly. 'Have you always wanted to "look after people", as they say?'

'Guess so,' she said lightly. She flicked a nervous look at the door—the others should be here soon. Somehow just Mike and herself in this room seemed a little too...intense. She was beginning to be wary of close encounters with this man!

'And you enjoy it?' he persisted.

'Yes, I love St Luke's. I just hope they don't shut

the place down. You've probably heard that a new hospital might be built outside town to replace this one. I love this job, though—feeling at the hub of things. I just wish the hours were better.'

He nodded and said casually, 'Hard when you've got family commitments, I guess.' He paused, then asked directly, 'Have you? I mean, are you married or do you have children?'

Lindy looked at him, startled, then smiled, a tight, controlled smile. '"No" to the first question. "No" to the second.'

Her brittle response wasn't lost on him. 'I'm sorry, I didn't mean to probe or appear nosy,' he said gently.

She reddened and bit her lip. Why on earth let him know that he'd touched a raw nerve—and why take it out on him just because of one dreadful experience? After all, not all men were like Jake...were they?

She rubbed the ridge of the old scar on her arm—a habit she'd developed over the years when she was tense. She had to put the past behind her, and learn never to be too trusting again.

Mike got up and swished his mug under the tap, looking back at her with a teasing look. 'I'm sure your life is very full anyway—a girl like you must have a pretty busy social life.'

Lindy brushed back a tendril of hair from her forehead. 'Never a dull moment,' she said brightly. 'And what about you—do you have commitments?'

'Sure I do—that's why I'd understand if you have a problem with the long hours. I know what it's like.'

Lindy looked at him curiously. What did he mean—commitments? Did he have a family of six and a demanding wife, or aged parents he had to look after?

She suddenly longed to find out.

'You have a wife and children then?' she asked tentatively.

He laughed. 'Nope—I'm fancy-free! But I doubt anyone would want to attach themselves to me at the moment with the baggage I bring with me. That's why an involving job is such a help—takes your mind off your worries when you're dealing with other people's problems, and, of course, meeting new colleagues…'

Those cobalt eyes held hers for a second, and Lindy felt her cheeks redden under that frank glance. She flicked a look at her watch, and spoke hurriedly to disguise any more interest in his private life. 'I'd better get back or Janet will be complaining that there aren't any nurses around and throw a strop.'

Mike chuckled. 'Oh, Janet's OK—a bit like a Rottweiler, but one that submits to training. She's got a lot on her plate—hospital management, understaffing and, of course, her brother.'

Lindy looked puzzled. 'What about her brother?'

'He's very disabled apparently and lives with Janet. He seems to have deteriorated recently and Janet's worried about his care.'

'I…I didn't know that,' murmured Lindy. She put the mugs back in the cupboard, slightly ashamed that most of them had never bothered to find out Janet's background situation. Mike had only been here a few days and already he knew more about her than anyone else! He had that endearing quality of taking time to listen to people, and Janet had obviously felt able to unburden herself to him rather than to staff she'd known for much longer.

His bleeper went off shrilly and he picked up the nearest phone. Janet's clipped tones came down the line. 'We have a two-year-old boy in with a scald to his chest in the burns room. Can you see how bad it is?'

Mike pulled a face as he put the phone down. 'Hate burns, especially in children. Rather do a pneumothorax any day…'

They could hear loud crying as they went down the corridor, although when they went into the special room set aside for burns the little boy was lying silently on the bed. It was his mother who was sobbing, her knuckles pressed into her mouth, staring at the child's injury. She looked about eighteen, with matted greasy hair and torn cut-off jeans. Both mother and child looked dirty and unkempt, and there were small encrusted blisters round the girl's mouth.

Carrie stood beside the young mother, an arm of comfort round the girl's thin shoulders.

'The little boy's called Ben, and his mum's Tessa Boardman,' she explained.

'It wasn't my fault.' Tessa's voice was high and hysterical. 'I just went next door to see someone. I weren't long…'

'Let's just look at the little lad first before we hear the details,' said Mike calmly, pulling on some sterile gloves.

Lindy turned on the overhead inspection light, and bent it over Ben's scrawny little chest. The T-shirt he'd been wearing had been cut away, revealing a scalded area that was a brilliant red and stretched from one side of his chest to the other. Large blisters had formed across the middle of the chest, and some of the superficial skin had shrivelled and rolled away, exposing engorged tissue underneath.

'He's got a bad partial burn and he's very shocked,' murmured Mike. 'Using the rule of nines, I'd say he's got a nine to twelve per cent burn. We need bloods for his blood urea and electrolyte count—and can you get a drip going, Sister? I'm going to ask Dr Bourne to come and look at Ben before we dress the injury.'

He went out to phone for the paediatrician, and Lindy quickly hooked up the saline bag to replace the liquids the child would have lost. She gently ruffled the little boy's matted hair. 'You'll be all right, Ben, pet. We're just going to put something over your chest to keep it clean and protect it.'

Ben watched Lindy silently, and when Mike returned allowed him to take blood from his arm with unnatural docility.

Dr Bourne came in, a short fat man with fluffy white hair and a kindly manner. He examined Ben's injury carefully, chatting to him gently all the time, then he turned to Mike. 'We'll give him two milligrams diamorphine, to keep him sedated and help with the pain.' He looked across at Tessa. 'Your son needs to stay in for a few days while we keep an eye on him. These burns are potentially dangerous, with the risk of infection, and we want to be extra careful.'

He nodded at Mike as he went out. 'See you in a minute, Dr Corrigan, when you've taken a full history.'

'So, tell us what happened, Tessa,' said Mike sitting down next to the young girl.

Tessa had stopped crying, but she looked frightened. 'He was all right when I left him,' she said defensively. 'I can't be everywhere at once, can I? He must have knocked over the coffee-jug on the stool.'

Her composure slipped again, her lips wobbling, and tears started to stream down her face. 'I didn't mean it, honest. I left him with his bottle. Usually he sits with it and doesn't move till I get back, but he must have pulled himself up on the stool and then…then the whole bloody lot's gone over him.'

Lindy took out the special dressing used for burns, and began spinning a mobile dangling from the ceiling filled with sparkling cardboard animals. Ben shifted his gaze and watched them revolve with big mournful eyes while Lindy prepared the Flamazine.

'You watch that pretty mobile, Ben—see how many animals you can see.' Lindy talked in a low, soothing voice to the child as she gently placed the dressing over the affected area.

Mike was still talking to Tessa. 'Exactly how long did you leave him for?' His voice had changed. It was tight and controlled, but Lindy heard undercurrents of tension that he didn't normally allow to show.

She looked up at him quickly. As far as Casualty was concerned, this case wasn't unusual. Many cases came in such as this one—a careless young mother and a frightening accident with grave repercussions. No matter how innocent the situation seemed to be, though, questions had to be asked. Perhaps Mike had his suspicions about this one. Lindy herself had already looked in the hospital files and they had no record that Ben had been a patient there before. She was inclined to believe the young girl's story—thoughtless rather than deliberate.

Tessa sounded sullen. 'I only left him for a minute, I swear. As I said, I've left him hundreds of times before, and he's been all right. Anyway, the coffee couldn't have been that hot—it had milk in it.'

Mike's voice had gained its equilibrium again, he sounded softer. 'I'm afraid the fat in the milk keeps its heat more than the water—it can make the situation worse. Now, tell me where you live.'

Tessa looked defensive again. 'I don't have to tell you that—it's nobody else's business. We…we've got a flat. I'm not having people nosing round after us!'

'As you like.'

Tessa shrugged sulkily. 'We live at Dock's End,' she said at last, looking at Mike and Lindy defiantly as if daring them to make some sort of moral judgement. Mike merely nodded. Everyone knew that area—a cluster of derelict sheds, and a base for vagrants, alcoholics and youngsters who'd left home. No place for a young girl to bring up a baby.

He made some notes, and Lindy turned to Carrie. 'Perhaps you'd take Tessa to the waiting room and give her a cup of tea.' She added quietly to the student nurse, 'Try and find out more about Tessa's circumstances in a relaxed atmosphere. Then perhaps we can get the hospital social worker onto her case. She needs help.'

Mike bent over Ben, looking closely at some sores on his face as Lindy applied more dressings to Ben's chest.

'I'm afraid Mum and son have a case of galloping impetigo to add to their woes,' he observed, straightening up. 'Even if we saturate them with antibiotics I don't see it disappearing for long. What on earth are they doing living in that dump anyway. The kid's got no chance there.'

His voice had that tense quality again, an underlying bitter note. Lindy looked at him, puzzled. She felt that more than ordinary compassion was bugging the man.

'He's not having a great start, that's for sure,' she admitted, 'but you don't think it was non-accidental injury, do you? It seemed just the sort of thing a thoughtless youngster like her might do—leave him, as she thought, for a minute or two.'

'You're probably right.' Mike folded his arms, staring at the ground. 'It's just another young life that'll go to waste—like his mother's.'

He sat down on a chair beside her and stroked the baby's hair gently. 'Why people have children when they can't look after them, I don't know.'

'She's only a kid herself,' Lindy reminded him gently. 'She's probably slipped the net and run away from home. The housing department must find her something better—she'll be a priority. Perhaps it's a good thing in the long run that Ben's been brought to our notice.'

Mike stood up abruptly and gave a short laugh. 'You're right—I'm not being very objective, am I?' He stared moodily into the distance. 'The trouble is, this scenario was a little close to home. My mother and sister were scalded badly by a kettle of boiling water. My father threw it at them in the middle of an alcoholic binge and my mother was virtually crippled for the rest of her life.'

Lindy stared at him in horror—no wonder Ben's case had touched a raw nerve.

'How…how terrible.'

The words sounded totally inadequate, but Mike shook his head. 'Usually I can keep a cool head, but today was…difficult. I shouldn't let it touch me—after all, what happened was a long time ago.' He patted Ben on the head. 'Goodbye, little fella—hope we don't see you back again.'

Lindy waited with the little boy until the porter came to take him to the paediatric ward. She felt shaken. Mike had revealed a shocking part of his past, a little window into his private life that told her that his surface confidence concealed unhappiness and tragedy. But, then, she thought wryly, who doesn't have some hidden heartache they'd rather put behind them?

Her heart hardened slightly. She wasn't going to feel sorry for the guy or let him slip under her guard—that way led to a broken heart.

CHAPTER THREE

LINDY'S legs were beginning to feel like very wobbly pieces of rubber—she hadn't taken any exercise like this for months. Faintly she wondered if the tachycardia she seemed to be experiencing was the prelude to a heart attack if she ran for much longer… She must have been completely mad to start on this regime anyway—and all because Mike had persuaded her to join the committee of the Save St Luke's appeal!

She lurched to a halt and leant breathlessly against a large oak luckily growing just by the path. The beautiful spring evening had persuaded her that now was a good time to start training for the fun run that was to be the first money-raising event. The air was cool and the grass had been cut for the first time, filling her nostrils with the sweet smell of new-mown hay.

She looked across the park, which stood high above the little town and from which she could see St Luke's Victorian building. It had to be worth saving—it was a real community hospital, with a wing for patients recovering from major operations and a rehabilitation ward for elderly people recovering from illnesses like strokes to prepare them for independent lives again. All the local population used it, and it was right in the centre of the town. It might be old, but it was a well-loved building, with its bright red brick and stone crenellations and topped by an enormous clock under which people arranged to meet.

She wondered crossly why on earth she had agreed

to join the committee when she had enough to do, working all day and looking after her little flat and the patch of garden that went with it. She'd been caught off guard, she reflected wryly, because Mike was too darned persuasive!

He'd asked her at the end of an exhausting afternoon—one of those days when the whole team had been stretched to breaking point and the pressure had been building up, culminating with three badly injured spectators caught in a fight outside a football match. All had needed blood transfusions and beds had had to be found in Intensive Care. Most of the day shift had sat sprawled around the kitchen, and Lindy had gratefully closed her eyes for a few minutes, trying to ignore her aching feet in the temporary lull.

'I've got a request.'

Through the haze of a pleasant daydream, Lindy's eyes flew open to find Mike looking down at her, a sheaf of papers in his hand. She blinked. She'd just been thinking of the man, and there he was, tall and broad, his fantastic eyes crinkling down at her and with a grin on his face!

Over the past few days her mind had irritatingly seemed to drift more and more around Mike Corrigan, no matter how much she tried to think of other things. Just the sight of his tall figure striding into a room and his deep blue eyes linking with hers sent her stomach fluttering, and she seemed to have a continual battle with her emotions. She'd been so wary of him to start with, but gradually he seemed to be getting under her defences—was it because of him that suddenly life seemed brighter, and the icy feeling round her heart had begun to fade?

He smiled beguilingly at her. 'Sorry to wake you up,

but we've just been discussing the impending doom of St Luke's, and everyone thinks you're the very person to come on the "Friends" committee to raise money to save the hospital!'

Lindy sat bolt upright, horrified at the notion. 'No—not me,' she pleaded. 'I'm not a committee sort of person. I'd be no good whatsoever—'

'Nonsense!' Mike did a treacherous thing—he bent down beside her so that his face was rather too close to hers, and his eyes with the dark flecks in their cobalt depths held hers rather too compellingly. 'Ray and Verity are too busy with their families, but you're not hampered by that sort of thing—so why not? It won't be very hard work, just a few ideas, a little organisation and one or two meetings—and I know you want to save the hospital!'

He sounded far too reassuring. Lindy looked at him suspiciously. 'I don't think I believe you about it not being hard work. When I finish at the end of the day, the last thing I want to do is go and talk about the hospital!'

'Nonsense!' Mike's voice was brisk. 'You'll find it great fun—I'll put your name down!'

'But—'

'No buts! And our first meeting's tomorrow night!'

'Are you on the committee?' she asked, a little surprised. Somehow she hadn't imagined that he was a committee person either.

'Of course,' he replied. 'We must do all we can to save a great institution like St Luke's—it's no good just paying lip-service to saving the place. I believe in giving one hundred per cent if something's worthwhile achieving—don't you?'

Lindy flushed slightly—she didn't want to appear

half-hearted. 'I suppose you're right,' she murmured. Reluctantly she conceded to herself that the idea of joining the committee sounded more attractive now that she knew he would also be on it!

And so she found herself attending the rather boozy meeting at the local pub, and helping to make the first decision—to have a fun run at the end of the month to start a summer of money-raising activities. And that was why she was now panting her heart out and wondering if she had overdone it. She hadn't realised she was quite so unfit, she thought mournfully. It looked as if the training would have to consist of more than the odd jogging session once a week!

'Hello! I see you're taking this very seriously!'

A loud, cheerful voice behind Lindy made her jump. She looked back breathlessly—she really didn't want anyone she knew to see her, red-faced and perspiring, her hair plastered wetly round her head and gasping like a fish out of water! She groaned inwardly as she recognised Mike bounding up the slope. He looked as if he made a habit of working out. He barely seemed out of breath—brief running shorts revealed strong, muscular legs pumping easily towards her. He wore a T-shirt over an impressively broad chest and a stars-and-stripes sweatband was pulled round his head. He looked tanned and healthy, exuding a kind of animal energy.

Lindy tried to slow down her breathing and not look like a total couch potato who'd suddenly dragged them-selves out of a chair and decided to run a mile—which was practically true! Thank heavens she'd elected to wear a faded but very baggy tracksuit that hid a mul-titude of sins. She tried to ignore the bounding of her heart which wasn't just to do with her laboured running.

'Just trying to get loosened up a bit,' she murmured. 'I find it's quite a good place to run.'

'Very impressive,' he observed, laughter in his eyes. 'You use this track a lot, then?'

'Not *this* track,' Lindy admitted cautiously, not actually lying but trying to give the impression that she wasn't a complete stranger to exercise. 'I'm just going back now to have a shower.'

To her dismay he turned round with her. 'We can both jog back together, then,' he said pleasantly. 'And then I think we've earned a large drink and a meal. What about it?'

Lindy felt a shock of surprise. The invitation was so unexpected—and alarming. It had obviously just been made on the spur of the moment, but she'd told herself it would be a long time before she went out alone with a man, especially a man she knew so little about. Let's face it—she didn't even know if she had the confidence to accept the most casual of invitations now.

'Not tonight,' she panted hastily. 'I've, er…things to do.' Like soaking in a hot bath all evening and drinking several glasses of wine after this evening of physical torture…

'Then we'll do it another night—say after your run tomorrow? We're both still on day shifts, I think.'

Mike's jogging was more like Lindy's running. It was hard to keep up with him, and impossible to carry on a conversation. It was all she could do to breathe… Perhaps that was why she gave in and blurted out, 'Fine!' It was easier than declining, and she had a feeling that Mike was the kind of man who'd persist until they found a mutually suitable date!

They finally came to the park gates. Gratefully Lindy clung to them as Mike trotted off briskly in the opposite direction.

'You can tell me where you live tomorrow and I'll pick you up at about seven,' he called as he disappeared at a tremendous rate down the high street. Lindy looked after him worriedly. What on earth had made her accept his invitation?

It had obviously been a bad Friday night in A and E. Trolleys still littered the passageway between the cubicles and the treatment rooms, and two huge oxygen cylinders were blocking the entrance to the ambulance bay. Lindy sighed. She needed Jack Hulse, the porter, but as usual he was difficult to find—probably having a quick smoke outside and discussing the football matches that afternoon with an ambulanceman.

She had enough on her mind, she thought crossly, without finding porters—namely, what should she wear tonight on her ill-advised date with Mike? Whenever she thought about the evening ahead her throat dried up with worry. It hadn't been so long ago when her last date with Jake had shattered her life completely, and she'd vowed to make it a very long time before she repeated the experience and went out with a man. The last thing on her mind at the moment was embarking on a new relationship with anyone. Then she shook herself mentally. She was making a mountain out of a molehill—the man had merely asked her out to supper, not for a weekend away. She would have a pleasant evening with Mike, which might lead to friendship—it didn't have to be anything else!

She pushed the trolleys into the cubicles and rang up the laundry to take a basket of dirty linen, then set off to find Jack, groaning when she saw Janet bearing down on her.

'Sister Jenkins! What on earth's happening here? Just how are we supposed to move emergencies through this clutter? You know the entrance is to be kept free at all times…'

One could always tell when Janet was especially cross when she used a formal title.

Lindy sighed. 'I know. I'm getting those cylinders moved pronto—that is, when I've found Jack. They're just a mite heavy to move by myself.'

'Make sure you do,' barked Janet.

Lindy marched purposefully off to find the porter. Being shouted at by Janet at the start of the shift wasn't a good omen, she thought gloomily. She felt a head-ache coming on.

Carrie came running up to Lindy when she returned to the central bay, her young face looking worried. 'Please, could you come? Ray's with that little girl— Miranda Fyles-Smith. She was the one with the broken arm at the beginning of the week…'

'And the mother with the charm bypass?' Lindy murmured with a grin. 'I didn't think she'd use this hospital again! What's the matter—is Miranda's plaster not right?'

'No. She looks really awful—having a bad attack of asthma. Her mother brought her in.'

'That's funny,' Lindy frowned. 'I don't remember anything like that in the history she gave us.'

Ray was standing outside the cubicle, looking flus-tered as usual. 'Mike's coming for this one in a minute. Could you start an assessment? I'm in the middle of removing a fish-hook from a boy's tongue—silly lad stood just behind his father as he was flicking the line. It's a bit tricky, really...'

He looked worriedly at Lindy, and she patted his shoulder soothingly. 'Don't worry, Ray, I'll cope—you can't save everyone at once!'

He scuttled off and Lindy went into the cubicle. With a quick but searching glance she took in the pallor of the plump little girl propped up in the cubicle bed. There was a tinge of blue about the child's lips and every few seconds she gave a wheezing cough.

Lindy picked up Miranda's wrist, feeling her galloping pulse rate, well over 140 a minute. There was hardly any need to listen to her chest—the wheezing, whistling sound of the choked-up lungs trying to expel air was perfectly audible.

Mrs Fyles-Smith's demeanour had changed dramatically since they had last met. She looked distraught, her mouth working, trying to stop herself from breaking down, and the immaculate hairdo and make-up had disappeared. She twisted her hands together as she watched her daughter fighting for breath.

'Please, help her,' she begged. 'She's been terrible all night—I've never known her be like this before. I thought she was being naughty, coughing and spluttering, but now....' Her voice trailed off into something very like a sob, and her daughter's eyes looked large with fear, as much at her mother's distress as at her own.

'Don't worry,' Lindy said in a firm voice, trying to calm the hysteria she could hear at the edge of Mrs Fyles-Smith's voice. 'You've done absolutely the right thing to bring Miranda in.' She pushed a large pillow behind the child, pulling the support forward so that she had to sit upright. 'We'll soon have her breathing easily again—and then you'll breathe easier too, I guess!'

She attached a pulse oximeter to the little girl's wrist and took a reading of her blood oxygen saturation and pulse.

Mike Corrigan swished through the curtains. 'I thought I could hear this young lady,' he said. 'You've got a few rattles in that chest of yours, haven't you?'

It was amazing the positive psychological effect a good medic could have on the patient—and on the nurse! thought Lindy. She flicked a grateful look at him as he dropped down beside the bed and smiled cheerfully at both mother and child. He just had to be everyone's idea of the ideal doctor—the confident manner and reassuring physical presence working a special wizardry of its own.

'We've got some good stuff that works like magic,' he assured them. 'Very soon I promise you that Miranda will be feeling pretty good.'

He turned to Lindy. 'What are her oxygen sats, Sister?' he enquired, as he listened to the little girl's chest through his stethoscope.

'Only 93 per cent,' she murmured quietly.

She took a mask hooked to the nebuliser machine beside the bed. 'See, Miranda, this machine makes magic bubbles that can make that horrid feeling in your chest disappear very quickly—I'll show you.'

She put the mask over her own face for a minute and Mike obligingly started the nebuliser. The child watched, fascinated, as the salbutamol started to bubble, and Lindy placed the mask over the little girl's face.

'One more magic thing, Miranda,' said Mike with a

grin, before she could protest about the mask. 'And we only do this on special people, you know!'

He looked meaningfully at Lindy. They had done this performance a few times that week, and she nodded understandingly. She took out a special teddy kept in most lockers for distraction purposes when needed. The teddy lay across her arm, and she produced a toy hypodermic, holding it up so that Miranda could see it.

'Teddy's feeling very breathless too,' Lindy explained. 'When I've given him this injection he's going to feel much better!'

Skilfully, she made the toy sit up suddenly as she gave the 'injection'. Miranda gave a chuckle of laughter and held her arm out for the bear. Mike's and Lindy's eyes met—the diversion had worked!

'And now it's your turn for the same medicine as Teddy,' said Mike cheerfully, quickly siting a venflon to allow him venous access.

'Miranda's having 100 mg of hydrocortisone,' he murmured to Lindy. 'And I want to check some blood gases.'

Lindy rubbed some local anaesthetic into the site Mike would use to take blood from the radial artery so that tests could be done. He took a syringe and felt for the radial pulse—it needed some skill to hit the vein precisely. He inserted the needle over the pulsation point and, gratifyingly, red blood spurted into the syringe at the first attempt.

'Bull's-eye.' He grinned. 'We should see a reaction pretty soon.'

Mrs Fyles-Smith looked on in relieved amazement as Miranda's colour returned and her breathing gradually became regular and easy.

'It's a miracle,' she breathed. 'She's improved in just a few minutes! Thank you so much!'

Suddenly the woman sounded almost human. Perhaps the sudden and terrifying onset of Miranda's asthma had made her realise just how precious her child was to her.

'Miranda's going to have to stay in for a night or two so that we can keep an eye on her,' explained Mike. 'I'll ring Paediatrics and see if they have a bed. I'm sure they'll arrange to run some allergy patch tests on her and see if we can pinpoint just what's started this. Is there anything she's done in the last few days that's been different to her normal life?'

The mother shook her head. 'It's a complete mystery. She didn't want to go to school two or three days ago—said she felt a bit off.' Mrs Fyles-Smith gave an uncomfortable laugh, and looked slightly shamefaced. 'I'm afraid I took no notice and made her go. She hadn't got a temperature or anything, and she's always saying she doesn't like school. I thought it was an excuse.'

Suddenly she looked as if she was going to cry again, and Lindy felt a stab of pity for her.

'Why don't you go and have a cup of tea?' she suggested. 'Have a break.'

Mrs Fyles-Smith nodded, and snapped open a compact from her handbag. Her hands were shaking as she held up the mirror to her face. 'God, what a mess,' she remarked in a firmer voice. 'I must just go and repair the damage, Nurse—and have a quick cigarette. It's OK…I know the rules! I'll go outside. You'll be all right for a minute, darling?'

Miranda nodded solemnly as her mother went out,

and watched Lindy for a moment. 'I won't have to go to school for a while, then?' she said suddenly.

Lindy grinned and said teasingly, 'Sorry about that. You'd like to get back as soon as possible, would you?'

'No…I hate it! I never want to go back!'

There was a vehemence about the child's voice that made Lindy turn round and look at her. 'Why not, Miranda?' she asked gently. 'What's so horrible about it?'

'I…I can't tell you…' Miranda's voice trailed off, and tears started to well out of her eyes and down her cheeks under the mask.

Lindy put her arms round the little girl. 'You can tell me anything, darling…anything at all. I won't be shocked—I might be able to help you.'

Miranda was silent, picking at the plaster on her broken arm. 'Nobody likes me,' she said at last in a tiny whisper. 'They really hate me there.'

Lindy looked at her seriously. Even if the child was imagining it, her fears were very real to her. 'How do you know that, love?'

'They call me Fatty and Big Legs and they pinch me. You know…I didn't fall off the slide the other day when I broke my arm—I was pushed.'

'Are you sure it wasn't an accident, Miranda?'

'I heard them say they were going to push me before. And the girl coming down behind me gave me a big shove with her legs. I…I was frightened to say anything.' Her voice wobbled and she hugged the teddy to her for comfort. 'And this week…this week they chased me into this horrible little shed in the playground. It was damp and dark. I was in there for ages until a teacher found me and let me out. It's where they keep all the gerbils and hamsters.'

Lindy hugged the child gently. 'Don't you worry, my pet. I'm sure when they hear that you've been ill, you won't have any more trouble. I'm just going out for one minute and I want you to lie back on that pillow and shut your little eyes for a moment. I know you're very tired.'

The child sighed, almost with relief, and closed her eyes. Lindy slipped out of the cubicle.

'What do you think, Mike—surely being shut up with those animals in a damp shed could trigger an allergy?'

Lindy had met Mike on his way back from phoning Paediatrics. 'It's certainly worth thinking about—and, of course, if she was terrified that could have started her hyperventilating,' he agreed.

He looked down at her with his smile to die for and a look of admiration in his eyes. 'She must trust you a lot, that little girl, to tell you about the bullying. We'd better have a word with the mother about that—she probably doesn't have an inkling of what Miranda's going through. I imagine Mrs Fyles-Smith doesn't have a very sympathetic ear.'

Lindy smiled impishly. 'I think having a talk to her can be your department—she seemed to take a shine to you the other day!'

He raised his eyebrows. 'You cannot be serious!' Then he caught her arm as she prepared to walk away. 'You haven't told me where you live—you haven't forgotten our date tonight, I hope?'

Lindy's heart thumped. Forgotten? It had been on her mind all day, a kind of excited apprehension at the thought of going out with a man other than Jake. No, not just any man—Mike Corrigan! She had to admit, she was beginning to warm to the idea. After all, who wouldn't look forward to a night out with someone so demonstrably kind, fun and good at his job—not to mention drop-dead gorgeous! Suddenly she felt a fizz of excitement that she hadn't known for months. Perhaps going for a meal might be rather fun after all!

'I'm the first terraced house in Laburnum Grove,' she said. 'It's just off the main road near the hospital.'

'I'll be there promptly at seven—be ready! I'm always on time!'

'Except when your bike's clutch or fuel line play up!' she murmured.

This was ridiculous! Lindy was beginning to feel like a teenager who'd never been on a date before, her heart fluttering with anticipation and nerves. For heaven's sake, she was just spending an hour or two with a colleague, wasn't she? They'd probably discuss the fundraising project for the hospital, his time in New York, nothing too deep. She thought she'd keep off the subject as to why he'd come back from abroad. It seemed as if she'd touched a delicate chord there—better to let him introduce that topic himself.

Lindy peered hopefully into her wardrobe and grabbed an armful of clothes, throwing them on the bed, then holding each outfit up against herself, looking critically in the mirror. They all looked horribly disappointing! When she'd been going out with Jake she'd been far too thin—he hated anyone to look, as he called it, 'bonnie'. Most of the time she'd gone out with him she seemed to have spent on rigorous diets which had often made her feel quite faint, existing mostly on low-cal soups and apples.

She'd made up for it since, she thought critically, gazing at herself in the mirror. In fact, it had been almost a relief in the past few weeks to eat what she wanted without feeling guilty. Sheila was always moaning to her how she envied Lindy her fantastic figure, with her long slender legs and generous bust that emphasised her small waist, but the clothes Jake had liked her to wear seemed far too skimpy now—she was shocked at the thought of how underweight she must have been to wear them. In the end she chose a pair of black trousers and a long-line pink jumper that flattered her curvy body—and the pink definitely suited her complexion, throwing up a glow on her cheeks.

Putting on make-up was a serious business—she didn't want to look tarty, but she needed some lift to her pale look after a day in Casualty. The smallest hint of blusher, a light shadow of beige on her eyelids and a warm pink on her lips... She scrutinised herself carefully in the mirror—that would have to do! She'd spent some time on her hair—it had a tendency to fly out in a mad halo if she didn't blow dry it firmly, and now it looked quite glossy and smooth in a thick dark bob. A quick spray of the lightest body spray she had, and she was ready!

Carefully she sat down on the sofa in her little lounge and looked at the clock. She'd timed it to perfection—just five minutes to go!

The phone call came just as Mike was about to leave the hospital. He'd been up to see Alfred Talbot after his operation. He always liked to find out what had happened to the patients one dealt with relatively briefly in A and E, and he wanted to know what chest injuries Mr Talbot had sustained after he'd treated his pneumothorax. Mr Gordon, the chest surgeon, was by the man's bed, checking his patients with the ward sister.

'How's he doing?' enquired Mike. 'What was causing the blood leak?'

Mr Gordon pursed his lips. 'It was a very small perforation in the aorta—the very devil to get at and, of course, it caused a major problem when you think of the heart pumping and the lungs trying to expand. As you might have guessed, there was tearing in the left lung as well. Fortunately we got it in time and Mr Talbot's doing very well. By the way, you did a good job on that drain, Mike!'

Mike walked briskly back to Casualty, pleased that the man had come through the ordeal so well. He glanced at his watch—he was looking forward to the evening and getting to know the voluptuous Lindy Jenkins better. He was amazed—and pleased—when he'd found out she wasn't married. Perhaps he'd discover what made her so intriguingly stand-offish when he'd arrived!

When his bleeper went off he went to the nearest phone to get the message. He hoped it wasn't a 999 call—he was due to finish at six o'clock and he wanted to prove to Lindy that he could arrive somewhere on time!

'Your sister on the line, Dr Corrigan.'

Mike tensed and groaned inwardly. Susy never rang him at work—something totally drastic must have happened for her to contact him.

'Sorry, Mike.' Her voice was high, frantic and panicky. 'I...I had to get in touch with you. It's Max, I think he's run away from home. I can't find him anywhere!' There was a pause, then with a breaking choke she gasped, 'Just suppose…just suppose he's gone off with…'

'I know what you're thinking, Susy,' Mike interrupted harshly. 'Put it out of your mind.' He forced his voice to sound level. 'I'll be with you in ten minutes—hang on. He can't have gone far!'

As he revved up his bike Mike's heart plummeted. An excitable and mischievous five-year-old like Max might be anywhere—or with anyone, especially if he knew that person well. At least, Mike thought grimly, accelerating down the high street, it vindicated him coming home from New York.

He flicked a look at the hospital clock as he whirled past, and cursed softly to himself—he hadn't got Lindy's number, and he hadn't got the time to find it out. He hated to let her down, and he didn't think she was the type of girl who'd take kindly to being messed about. In the short time they'd worked together, however, he thought he knew enough about her to know that in the situation he was in, she would understand why he had to put Max first.

It was nine o'clock. Lindy had sat in her little sitting room for two hours. At first she'd thought with amusement that Mike's bike had let him down again, then she'd decided that he would probably come in the little sports car she'd seen him park occasionally at the hospital.

Once the phone rang, and she rushed to answer it, convinced that Mike was ringing to say he'd been delayed—but it had been Sheila, ringing about Sunday lunch the next day. Lindy had asked if Mike had been delayed at the hospital, but Sheila had replied that she'd seen Mike leaving on his bike on time.

Finally Lindy decided that Mike was never going to show up. She went up to her bedroom, tearing off the black trousers and the pink sweater and throwing them viciously into a corner of the room. Why had she allowed herself to be conned into a meal with that jerk? she wondered bitterly. He was nothing but a carbon copy of Jake, a heart-stopping rat with nothing behind the façade. He'd treated her like dirt, not even having the good manners to let her know he wasn't coming. He'd obviously had something better to do with his time than take her out... She hurled her shoes after the clothes.

'I should have known you were just a good-looking louse who thought the world of himself. Well, goodnight and goodbye, Dr Corrigan! If you think I'm going to stay on that committee with you, you're very much mistaken. I know the score now and I'm giving you a wide berth—you're just like Jake after all!'

She collapsed on the bed and sobbed into her hands. Just as she'd begun to forget about the way Jake had treated her and build up her self-confidence, the wound had been ripped open again.

CHAPTER FOUR

THE phone rang shrilly by Lindy's ear, dragging her abruptly from the deepest sleep she'd had in a restless night. It took a second for her to marshal her jumbled thoughts—what time was it, what *day* was it even? Then, with a sudden sickening flash, last night's debacle came back to her. Her heart started hammering. It just had to be Mike, ringing, no doubt to give some explanation about his non-appearance last evening.

She snatched up the receiver. After a night tossing and turning, she wondered if perhaps she'd been too harsh on the man. She'd likened him to Jake last night, because that had been the kind of thing Jake would have done—let her down without explanation. But Mike was very different in manner—he had a warmth and humour that Jake had never had. Was it just possible that he had a good reason for leaving her high and dry last night?

But it wasn't Mike's deep voice on the end of the line. Lindy's heart sank slightly as Janet's brusque tones hit her ears loudly and tersely. It had to be some sort of an emergency.

'Lindy—we're in a pickle. Sheila's phoned in sick now, and we've a multiple RTA coming in. Sunday's a bad day, but is there any chance of you helping us out? I know it's Verity's job to ring you, but she's running round in circles at the moment.'

Lindy sighed. Days off were precious—but what did it matter? She'd probably just spend the day going furiously over her broken date, and the lunch Sheila had asked her to was obviously off anyway if she was ill. When road traffic accidents occurred, the hospital was always very stretched.

'I'm on my way, Janet,' she said resignedly. 'Give me ten minutes.'

The driveway in front of A and E was jammed with four ambulances and a police car with its blue light still flashing. Lindy braced herself for the chaos she knew she'd find inside.

The corridor was completely full of trolleys—there must have been at least ten, each with a figure lying on it, some groaning, some ominously still. Lindy recognised quite a few staff from Medical who'd obviously been brought in for the emergency, setting up drips and swabbing wounds in the limited space of the unit. Even Janet looked frazzled, her normally brisk manner slightly off-key, feeling her way, as one often had to when there was an overwhelming accident.

Her face cleared slightly at Lindy's appearance. 'Thanks, Lindy, I appreciate this. Apparently a party of fourteen cyclists was run into by a horsebox which lost control on a hill. The first patient's gone into the small theatre—could you start getting bloods for cross-matching, and doing his obs? He's got multiple fractures, probable broken femur, possible internal injuries.'

The patient was young—late teens, Lindy guessed. His short, dark hair was matted with dried blood from a gash on his forehead, a collar was round his neck and a drip connected to his arm. There was something awkward and contorted about the angle of his right leg on the bed, and Lindy pursed her lips in sympathy. It didn't need much imagination to guess the amount of pain the boy was in.

A tall figure was bent over the boy's body, listening to the patient's chest. He looked up, his eyes meeting Lindy's in a grim judgement of the injuries. Even allowing for the stress in dealing with the accident, Mike looked terrible. His face was almost as grey as the patient's, and tired lines were etched in the corners of his eyes. Lindy looked at him sharply. Just what had happened to the man since she'd last seen him the day before? She shrugged inwardly—now was not the time to wonder about that.

His glance held hers for a second and she thought they held a shadow of contrition, but his voice was upbeat, professional, revealing no other emotion except immediate concern for his patient.

'Hello, Sister. This is Carlo Romoli—had an argument with a horsebox and the horsebox won. I suspect Carlo's got a broken femur, and compound fracture of his tibia, with a Pott's fracture of his fibia. We'll need venous access for analgesia and detailed X-rays, including the spine. Mark Hadfield's coming down from Orthopaedics to look at Carlo prior to operating on him.' He smiled compassionately at the young man. 'Can't be very comfortable, Carlo, but we'll do something about that pronto. Five milligrams of diamorphine should help you to feel more human.'

Carlo groaned and sucked in his breath. 'Feel pretty terrible?' said Lindy sympathetically as she injected the diamorphine.

'Yup!' muttered the boy. He looked at her mournfully. 'Worse than that—it was a new bike—got it for my eighteenth birthday from Mum and Dad. They're going to be gutted when they find out what's happened to it!'

Lindy smiled wryly at him. 'I don't think it's the loss of your bike they're going to worry about somehow!' She talked gently to him as the diamorphine took effect. 'You've got a lovely name—where does your family come from? Your English is perfect.'

'My parents are Italian, but we've moved around a lot, lived on and off in English-speaking countries for years.'

'Where are your parents now?' she asked.

'In London—I'm at college up here.'

'The police will let them know what's happened to you,' Lindy said. She turned to Jack, who had just appeared at the doorway. 'Treat this young man like crystal when you take him to X-ray, Jack—very gently round the corners, please!'

Jack nodded and trundled Carlo off for his X-rays.

Lindy started to tidy up the cubicle, the hairs on the nape of her neck standing up, intensely aware of Mike standing behind her and the tension that crackled in the atmosphere. She wasn't going to mention last night— why reveal that his rudeness meant anything to her on a personal level at all, although anger at his cavalier treatment of her made her blood boil. Then suddenly she felt his firm touch on her arm, and her pulse rate increased with a bound as he turned her round to face him.

He tilted her face towards his with his finger under her chin, and she was forced to meet his gaze. 'Can you forgive me for standing you up last night, Lindy? I owe you an apology,' he said quietly. 'You know that nothing would have made me miss our date unless something pretty profound had happened, don't you?'

She tried to subdue the stab of sympathy going through her at the sight of his haggard face, despite her wounded feelings. Yesterday evening she had vowed not to listen to any excuses—now she felt herself wavering slightly. Whatever had prevented Mike from coming round last night seemed to have aged him ten years. Then she bit her lip and shook herself mentally. Surely she wasn't going to give in and fall for the sympathy ticket, letting him off the hook just because he looked miserable? When he hadn't turned up she'd been reminded very forcibly that having a relationship meant letting your defences down. If she let someone get close to her, she'd only ended up getting hurt. Far better to keep her emotions in check…

'Not to worry,' she said coolly. 'The TV was pretty good and I got some tidying up done.' Tidying up of the clothes she'd thrown in the corner of her bedroom, she thought ruefully.

'I would have rung you,' he said, 'if circumstances had given me more time…'

'Sure,' she interrupted lightly. 'It's no problem. Excuse me.' She pushed passed him and he dropped his hand from her arm as Janet came briskly through the door.

'Ah!' Janet said with satisfaction, noting the empty room. 'You finished with your fracture patient?'

Mike nodded. 'Gone for X-rays prior to surgery. He's in a bit of a mess, but he's maintaining adequate BP and oxygen saturation.'

'Right, I'm afraid we're still in chaos, and we're hunting for free theatres. Can you and Sister use this small theatre to patch up John Ludlam, the driver of the horsebox? He's got a nasty laceration on his neck and forehead where a broken wing mirror managed to make contact in the collision. It's not a large gash, but it's gone as deep as the periosteum, so it'll need careful alignment and stitching. He's being brought back from Theatre as there wasn't any room for him.'

It was Sod's Law, reflected Lindy wryly, that she and Mike were spending most of the morning together working as a team, when their personal relationship seemed to be on quicksands! She brought forward the instrument tray and checked the delicate instruments that Mike would need for the minute and precise facial surgery he'd have to perform—the splinter-fine needles, miniature forceps and filament-like catgut. She could hear Mike scrubbing up in the little anteroom, and a minute later he appeared gowned and masked, his head covered with a jay-cloth hat.

Lindy glanced at him under her lashes, and her heart danced a sudden crazy rhythm against her ribs. Mike could have stepped straight out of a TV hospital drama! He looked the perfect surgeon—tall and broad, the open ties of the gown showing his strong neck with a cluster of dark hairs at their base, and cobalt eyes fringed with black lashes gazing at her over his mask. She could tell he was smiling at her from the way his eyes crinkled up as they met hers.

'As I was saying before we were so rudely interrupted,' he murmured wryly, 'I'm not a total bastard, you know. I would have done anything to get in touch, but I didn't have your number to hand, and there wasn't time—'

'I told you, it's of no consequence.' Lindy kept her voice light. He looked so disturbingly attractive she had to keep reminding herself that the man had actually stood her up. She found herself longing to shout 'I forgive you' and put comforting arms around him.

His eyes narrowed over the mask. 'You *do* think the worst of me, don't you? You think I just forgot to come—didn't give a damn about you?'

'I did *not*...' Lindy flushed. 'Well, perhaps a phone call would have helped.'

'I know.' His voice was contrite. 'That's why I'm taking you out after this to explain.' He stepped a little nearer and looked down at her intensely. 'I'd never want you to think I'm unreliable.'

She shook her head firmly. 'I'm afraid I'm too busy at the moment to—'

Mike put a gloved hand up. 'No buts—the surgeon can't be interrupted! Here comes Mr Ludlam anyway.'

There wasn't time to argue. Mr Ludlam was plainly in shock, his skin sweating and grey. A drip was attached to his arm to offset the effects of shock, but his expression was distraught.

He grabbed Lindy's hand. 'Tell me what's happened,' he whispered hoarsely. 'Nobody will tell me anything.' He looked pleadingly up at her. 'The brakes failed. I don't know why, but I felt the whole vehicle veer over to the side and it just slid into them—all these young lads! Have I killed any of them? I can't bear it if I have... I was going to pick up a horse, you see...'

His voice broke and he turned his face miserably to one side. Lindy and Mike's eyes met in mutual sympathy.

'Our Casualty Officer, Dr Lessiter, tells me that no one's been killed, Mr Ludlam,' Mike said firmly. 'As soon as we have some more concrete information we'll let you know.'

He sat down on a chair and shone a bright torch on the patient's forehead wound, looking carefully to see if the membrane that covered and nourished the bone had been broken. He nodded with satisfaction when he found it still intact.

'You've got a nasty gash on your forehead and neck which I'm going to repair. You'll need some local anaesthetic which I'll inject now—it takes away all sensitivity to pain.'

'Does it stop you feeling like a murderer, Doc?' whispered Mr Ludlam.

Mike laid a comforting hand on the distressed man's shoulder—a gesture not lost on Lindy. Physical touch was an incredibly important and soothing thing to someone as tormented as John Ludlum. His scars would heal quickly, but the mental anguish of what had happened would stay with him for ever—whether it had been his fault or not.

'The accident might be nothing to do with you,' said Mike quietly. 'I'm sure the police will run thorough checks on the vehicle. Now, try to relax whilst I start on this wound.'

Lindy watched Mike working with admiration—it was a delicate job to close the frontalis muscle of the forehead and any misalignment could cause a facial distortion. He worked quickly and ably, cutting away any crushed tissue round the wound and then, when he had finished, stitching it with the fine filament gut Lindy passed him in the threaded needle.

At last Mike finished, and he stood back with a relieved sigh, pulling off the latex gloves he'd used and flinging them into the bin together with his mask.

'There you are, Mr Ludlam—I don't think I've ruined your looks. You'll be taken to a cubicle to recover now, but I'm afraid the police are here to question you about the accident. Do you think you can cope with that?'

The man nodded miserably. 'Thanks, Doc. I'd like to get it over with,' he muttered tonelessly.

After a feverish day, in which the whole team seemed never to have had time to draw breath, Lindy stepped out into the soft spring afternoon sunshine filtering down on the lawn to the side of the hospital. She inhaled the sweet air with relief, stretching her arms to try and relax the tension of the past few hours. It had been hectic, but despite the shortage of staff they'd all pulled together well—even she and Mike had forgotten any awkwardness between them as they'd worked desperately to stabilise broken bodies and calm hysterical relatives.

A sudden dart of anxiety went through Lindy as she remembered Mike's undertaking to explain to her after work what had happened the night before. Did she want that explanation—or was it better to walk away now and stop any more contact with him before she felt the web of attraction closing in on her again?

It was too late. Ruefully, she knew without turning round that the brisk steps behind her belonged to Mike. He looked a different man, dressed almost identically to her in jeans and a loose white shirt. He smiled down at her.

'I'm glad you didn't think of running away before I had a chance to talk to you.'

Lindy felt her cheeks flush—he was rather close to the truth! She pushed a lock of hair behind her ear. 'How long will this explanation take?' she enquired rather baldly.

'As long as it takes to have some ice-cold lemonade and home-made cake!'

She looked at him curiously. 'You make cake?'

'My sister does—she never eats it herself, so I have the benefit! We both need a break, so let me drive you to my home. I'll bring you back here later.'

What should she do? Lindy's thoughts whirled like ingredients in a mixer. Somehow she guessed this was the decisive moment—should she keep her distance and go home, or go with him and allow the little tendrils of attraction to wind more treacherously round her heart? He looked at her, waiting for her answer, a slightly amused quirk to his lips that seemed to say he knew what was going through her mind! Damn it, she really *was* curious to know why he'd never turned up, and why he looked so exhausted—and, yes, she'd love to see Mike in his own surroundings!

She made an effort to keep her distance. 'Can't you tell me here?' she asked. 'I'm really tired…'

'I can't describe how refreshing iced lemonade is,' he coaxed. 'And the chocolate cake is as light as a feather!'

She gave a sudden tired laugh. 'OK, you win! It sounds too tempting to resist! Just for a short while, though…'

Some houses just seem so *right,* thought Lindy with delight, looking at the picture-postcard cottage that was Mike's home. Its thatched roof and pretty spring garden with daffodils, jonquils and crocuses set in the countryside just outside Manorfield looked like something the English Tourist Board might have used in an advertisement for a fairy-tale holiday.

'Oh,' she breathed, forgetting for a moment her apprehension about being alone with Mike. 'What a wonderful place—is it yours?'

'I wish,' sighed Mike, opening the front door. 'I rent

it at the moment, but I'm hoping I'll get the option to buy soon—the owner is trying to make up his mind whether to live abroad or not.'

They stood in the dark little hallway and he switched on a light. Lindy felt a knot of apprehension bunch up in her stomach—it was just a little too intimate. Mike's tall frame was slightly too close to be comfortable. He'd had a shower at the hospital after the busy morning and she could smell the clean, soapy smell of him, the warmth of his breath on her face. Crazily she felt that if someone threw a switch, the crackle of tension between them would ignite and she'd spring towards him like a magnet to metal! She gave a shaky laugh to break the silence.

'What about this refreshing lemonade and cake, then?'

'Of course—follow me.'

Ducking his head under the low doorway, he led her into an enchanting room with large bow windows looking out over the garden and the fields and hills beyond. The furniture was in perfect keeping with the cottage— chintzy covers on cosy armchairs, and a little bureau bookcase filled with books by the wall.

Lindy sat on a window-seat and waited while Mike disappeared into the kitchen. It was like being in a film set, she thought, it was so perfect. She picked up a photo from a little table. It was quite old, black and white, and showed a young boy of about ten and a little girl—obviously brother and sister. They looked solemnly—even sadly—into the camera, and Lindy frowned. The boy had a familiar look—surely she'd known someone like that once? Then she smiled to herself. Of course! The boy was the young Mike, with skinny long legs and a round youthful face, and it was familiar because she knew him now.

Lindy studied the photograph more closely. Mike had his arm protectively flung round his little sister, and Lindy was suddenly reminded of Mike's terrible story about the consequences of his father's drinking. She would guess that his childhood had not been a happy one and the faded picture did have an aura of sadness about it, as if the two youngsters were somehow pitted against the rest of the world. In the background could be seen a large house with a veranda running round it and French windows in the middle.

Lindy reflected that it was similar to a house she'd once known, long ago and now half-remembered. Something horrid had happened to her there when she was very young, and the flashback she sometimes experienced formed before her eyes—she was falling through the glass of a door, blood was pouring out of her arm and she was feeling very frightened... She closed her eyes briefly and pushed the thought away firmly.

She put the photo down. She was always thinking that places and faces were familiar from the past—perhaps because she wanted to find out more about her own family and where she was from. She shrugged and smiled rather bleakly to herself. With any luck perhaps she would be finding out about her background fairly soon. Despite her misgivings as to whether she was doing the right thing to find out about her past, she had put all the wheels in motion. Any day now she expected a letter that would help her to open the door to her early childhood.

Mike returned with a tray, setting it down on the table, and poured her a large glass of lemonade, then cut her a generous slice of a mouth-watering chocolate cake filled with butter icing.

'Instant energy,' he remarked. 'After the morning we've had, you need it.'

He passed her a plate and Lindy couldn't resist sinking her teeth into the soft, moist centre of the cake immediately, revelling in the smooth texture of the butter icing.

'Mmm—I don't care what this does for my cholesterol, it's ambrosial!' she murmured. 'Your sister sure can bake!'

He watched her with amusement, his sexy blue eyes laughing at her attempt to chew more than she could, and Lindy laughed back at him after she'd finished a large mouthful. Then suddenly she remembered why they were there, and put down her plate abruptly. Was Mike trying to put off the moment to tell her what had happened, softening her up with delicious food?

'So,' she said sternly, 'just what *did* prevent you coming last night? Was it an emergency so fraught that you couldn't phone me?'

His expression changed, and he sat down beside her and gazed out of the window for a second. 'It was an emergency all right.' He spoke slowly, his voice heavy. 'But it wasn't the hospital this time. It was something nearer to home and to do with my family—very boring, I'm afraid, as family dramas usually are.'

Lindy looked at his set profile and the worried frown that lined his forehead, and another flash of sympathy darted through her. He seemed very protective of his family—she had seen that in the old photograph of him as a child. Her mind seethed with curiosity. Was the man going to tell her what had happened without her prising it out of him? It was obviously something he felt reluctant to talk about, but she just *had* to know!

'Was someone ill?' she asked delicately.

He shook his head. 'My family is very complicated,' he said at last. 'My sister is a single parent and her ex-husband is a complete rat. I won't go into everything he's done to her, but he's a very nasty piece of work.'

'But they are divorced?'

'Yes, thank God, and Susy has custody of Max, their little son. Rick only has access to him at specified times when Susy is there at the same time. This doesn't go down well with Rick. Several times he's tried to take Max—last night he tried again, and almost succeeded.'

Lindy looked at Mike speechlessly, then eventually found her voice. 'But that's *terrible*. Are the police involved?'

He shook his head in something like despair. 'I know it's unbelievable, but Susy doesn't want the police involved—yet. She still seems to feel something for this ghastly man and a court order might deny him any access to Max at all, and she does want the little boy to see his father.'

'So that was where you were last night—rescuing Max?'

'Until about two in the morning,' he admitted. 'Max disappeared after playing outside in the garden, and my sister was frantic that Rick had taken him and might smuggle him out of the country. Luckily they'd only got as far as Rick's flat, and I was finally able to persuade him that Max had to be with his mother…but it wasn't easy.'

Mike ran long fingers through his hair so that it stood up in spikes round his head, and Lindy guessed that what he'd described had been an understatement of the facts.

He smiled ruefully at her. 'I can tell you I'd much rather have been wining and dining you, Lindy, than dashing round the back streets of Manorfield at dead of night.' He leaned forward, his eyes looking deep into hers. 'So, am I forgiven, then?'

How could she not forgive him? That beseeching look, the rueful half-smile on his firm mouth... It had been a frightening story, and Lindy resisted the temptation to smooth down his rumpled hair and lay a comforting cheek against his. She half shut her eyes. She could almost feel the rough texture of his chin against her own soft skin, and the thickness of his hair through her fingers... Then she swallowed and took a deep breath. Mike had asked her out purely on a friendly basis, and she had to suppress these quite ridiculous feelings of physical attraction for him.

'Of course it wasn't your fault... I'm so glad you managed to find your nephew—your sister must have been incredibly relieved.'

'She was rather,' he said with a wry smile. 'It was a harrowing experience, though. As you can imagine, Max is a very confused little boy at times, and seeing both his parents in a very emotional state doesn't help things. To be honest, I wish Susy could cut herself off completely from Rick.'

'Don't you think Max needs to know his father?'

Mike's expression hardened. 'Quite frankly, whatever my sister thinks, he's a carbon copy of my own father, and the best thing that happened in *my* childhood was when he disappeared for good! Sometimes one's better off without parents!'

'Do you think so?' Lindy smiled rather sadly at him.

Everyone had a different point of view, of course, but she rather thought she would have done anything to find out more about hers—the young mother who'd put her up for adoption all those years ago. She pushed the familiar ache of wanting to see her to the back of her mind.

'You must be very fond of the little boy. Was he the commitment you came back from New York for?'

Mike's face lit up. 'Ah, he's a great kid—fun, energetic, cheeky. You'd love him! And, yes, I couldn't let my sister flounder with a child on her own. She needed my support, and it was no hardship at all to do that for them.'

Lindy nodded. Of course, someone like Mike would take his responsibilities towards his sister very seriously. Somewhere, however, niggling deep down in the recesses of her mind was the thought that his sister and her son would always come first in any relationship. Next time she fell for someone, Lindy thought grimly, she would want to be a priority in their affections—not a sideline.

There was a short silence, then he stood up and took her hand, pulling her up beside him. 'Now you know the whole story, and perhaps you and I can start again,' he said quietly. He kept hold of one hand and gently touched her shining dark hair. 'Will you allow me to make it up to you?' he murmured.

She looked up at him and, despite her misgivings, was electrified by his sudden touch. If only he hadn't got such deep blue eyes…if only his mouth wasn't quite so sexy and firm…the clean soapy male smell of him so close…

'There's really no need…' Lindy murmured weakly.

His face lit up with a sudden grin, making him look

younger, more boyish. 'That's all right, then,' he murmured, and brushed a gentle kiss across her parted lips.

It was like a bolt of lightning, the red-hot flame of
desire that licked treacherously through Lindy's body.
Almost as if he'd pressed an erogenous-zone button,
her responses leapt into gear, her mouth opening lan-
guidly to his, her body arching against him as his hands
slowly swept over her curves. Then his arms folded
strongly round her, and they were locked together, hip
to hip.

Somewhere in Lindy's befuddled brain, through the
intoxication of the feel of that hard body on hers, panic
and guilt at the unexpected intimate physical contact
shuddered through her. What on earth did she think she
was doing—answering a gentle pass with such an eager
answer? Her first instincts had been right—she should
never have come to his house.

The sweet touch of his firm mouth on her lips had
triggered the most incredible and unsuitable response.
Oh, yes, she couldn't deny that she had, over the past
few weeks, dreamt of Mike doing wonderful things to
her, his mouth demandingly against hers, his arms
round her body, pressing her close to him, and she
returning those kisses with fervour. But that had been
in the safety of dreams over which she had no control,
and the reality shamed and terrified her! Terrified her
that the whole thing was getting out of hand, gathering
speed, and that she would fall for him totally and be
unable to get off the roundabout. She couldn't bear
another Jake scenario again.

Somehow she pulled herself away from his demanding body, her hair tousled and cheeks flushed. Breathlessly she brushed back stray locks of hair behind her
ear, and straightened her T-shirt.

'I…I must go,' she stammered frantically, but trying to inject a light tone into her voice. Her heart pounded like a piston engine. 'It's been lovely, and I think the cottage is fantastic, but I have so much to do. I'll just use your bathroom before we go.'

He stepped back and looked at her quizzically for a second. Then he said easily, with a little crooked smile, 'Sure, up the stairs and on your left. Then I'll take you back.'

Mike's eyes watched her as she left the room, suppressing a longing to follow her and fold her in his arms again. He'd never thought he'd feel such a profound attraction for a girl—and he'd had many who'd given him every encouragement. He was no monk, but no one had moved him like Lindy Jenkins. She was so beautiful—a complexion like a peach, those large expressive sherry-coloured eyes and a body to die for. And he could feel without a doubt the crackle of attraction between them, although they'd known each other such a short time. He frowned angrily to himself. He'd rushed her too quickly. His tendency to be impulsive had often got him into trouble in the past.

He was exasperated and yet intrigued by her inhibitions. There was some demon in her past, he sensed, that prevented her from giving herself completely. He would have to play it very cool, take it slowly. Somehow, someday, he would find out what that past had been, what she was so frightened of, and try and heal those emotional scars.

CHAPTER FIVE

THE bouncy castle was doing great business. A crowd of children were lined up, desperate to fling themselves about in it, and the air was filled with excited shrieks and screams.

'That's a sure recipe for a stream of youngsters to come into Casualty with concussion and fractured skulls,' observed Janet gloomily.

She and Lindy were manning A and E's information stall on the opening day of the Save St Luke's appeal which would culminate in a fun run round the hospital grounds and park. Lindy chuckled to herself—trust Janet to be pessimistic! She'd already made dire predictions about the run and how many wrenched ankles they'd get!

'It seems to have attracted lots of people,' Lindy remarked, looking round at the marquee erected on the side lawn of the hospital for refreshments, and the tubs of spring flowers along the terrace. The sun was quite warm and there was a general air of carnival about the place.

She had put on her standard nurse's uniform with the St Luke's traditional winged nursing cap perched on her head, feeling that the trousers and tunic top would be too hot on a day like today. She felt a little self-conscious—it would have been nice to have worn something ordinary and summery. As it was, she would have to be quick changing into her fun-run gear after her stint on this information stall.

A shiver of apprehension ran through her at the thought of this so-called 'fun' run—anything but fun, she groaned to herself, feeling guilty about the lack of training she'd had. And wasn't that all Mike's fault? She had been just too nervous of meeting him by chance again on a practice jog after work—she felt a flush of shame and embarrassment every time she thought about her eager response to him at his cottage, and had not wanted to risk seeing him outside the hospital. If she collapsed on the track through being unfit, it would be his fault entirely!

She had to admit that although she did her best to push them out, her thoughts were too often of Mike these days. It had been a total shock at the cottage to find out just how attracted she was to him. She wasn't ready for that yet—she couldn't allow herself to spin headlong into a relationship that could very well end in a broken heart again. Only a few weeks ago, when she had finally found out the truth about Jake, she had been devastated and had vowed it would be a long time before she allowed herself to fall for someone else. How could she have allowed herself to respond so easily to another man so soon?

She had tried very hard to keep out of Mike's way, but it hadn't stopped her being intensely aware of him at work, and dreaming wonderful sexy dreams about him at night!

Fiercely she banished all thoughts about Mike from her mind, and turned her attention to demonstrating the measurement of blood pressure with a sphygmomanometer, using Carrie as a patient, before a little knot of onlookers. An earnest young reporter, who was covering the event for the local newspaper, asked a barrage of ghoulish questions about the most serious kind of injuries Casualty had to deal with, and just how important the hospital was to the local community.

'You can tell how much people think of St Luke's by the crowd that's here supporting the hospital,' Lindy pointed out.

'And I'd just like to say that my daughter has had superb treatment twice in one week—St Luke's has literally been a life-saver for her,' said a drawling voice that was vaguely familiar.

In front of the stall stood Mrs Fyles-Smith with Miranda! Lindy tried to hide her astonished look. She just hadn't imagined that someone like her would bother to come to a fund-raising do for anything as boring as the hospital—surely high-powered charity lunches and balls were more her scene!

'Thank you for supporting St Luke's appeal.' She beamed at Miranda and her mother. 'Have you been well, Miranda? Your plaster will be coming off soon, won't it?'

The little girl certainly looked better—more relaxed, pink-faced and smiling. She looked at her mother proudly. 'Mummy's going to do the fun run to help raise money,' she informed Lindy.

Lindy looked with renewed astonishment and respect at Mrs Fyles-Smith. The woman had hidden depths!

A flush of slight embarrassment crossed Mrs Fyles-Smith's face. 'You helped Miranda so much, finding out about the school bullying situation and everything. I was...very grateful.'

Lindy tried not to let her jaw drop open as the woman continued off-handedly, 'I work out every day at this ghastly fitness centre place, so I thought I might manage to totter round the course. When Dr Corrigan told me about the desperate straits the hospital was in, I felt I had to do my bit... We must try and save it.'

Lindy met Janet's eyes and bit her lip to suppress her amusement. 'That's great. Thank you so much,' she said gravely.

Mike could certainly work his magic on women, she reflected wryly. But, then, he was a very charming and persuasive man. Lindy watched the mother and daughter wander over towards the park, Mrs Fyles-Smith dressed appropriately in Lycra running shorts and an expensive sweatshirt, her feet sporting the latest designer running shoes. Who would have thought that someone like that woman would have cared about what happened to the hospital—she had seemed so hardbitten and self-absorbed. Mike had obviously managed to nudge her conscience!

'Excuse me, Nurse,' murmured a deep voice, 'but could you tell me if it's true that the staff in Casualty have to work a twenty-four-hour day with no breaks and only one doctor and nurse on hand to deal with hundreds of casualties?'

Lindy whipped round, the unexpected sound of that voice sending something like a whole roomful of butterflies fluttering through her stomach! She had thought Mike was far away in the park, helping to organise the running event, and it was a shock to find the subject of her daydream standing beside her, looking pretty devastating in a grey tracksuit with the words SAVE ST LUKE'S emblazoned in red across the front! She gulped, and gave him a cool little nod—he wasn't going to give him the impression that he meant anything more to her than a colleague. But Janet Lessiter smiled broadly at his arrival.

'Quite often the staff are on the edge of nervous

breakdowns, aren't they, Nurse?' Janet added with a wink at Lindy, amplifying Mike's startling remarks about Casualty. Despite her tension at Mike's appearance, Lindy gave an inward giggle—it wasn't often one got a joke from Janet!

The young reporter came eagerly forward, pencil poised over his notebook, hoping for a scoop on the staff situation at the hospital, and Mike grinned and shook his head at the young man.

'Only a joke, I'm afraid. I think A and E's in control most of the time!'

The reporter looked at Mike's name badge, shrugged his shoulders and ambled off good-naturedly.

Lindy laughed. 'You'll probably have us all hauled before the health authority now!'

'That I'd like,' declared Janet grimly. 'I could tell them a thing or two about staffing at this hospital!' She looked at Lindy. 'You're due to do this ridiculous run, aren't you? Off you go, then. Sheila's going to come in a minute to help out, and I don't need too many of you! And don't come back cluttering up the beds as a patient,' she added brusquely.

'Good idea,' said Mike, looking down at Lindy sternly. 'You ought to start doing some warming-up exercises anyway—I haven't seen you in training much. In fact,' he added softly, 'I haven't seen you much at all. You did promise that we could have that evening out together, didn't you, to make up for the mess I made of our other date? I'd like to keep you to that! I'm free tonight!'

He flung a casual arm round her shoulders and began to walk towards the park.

'I never promised anything...' began Lindy breathlessly, trying to ignore the delicious sensation of his warm arm holding her just slightly too firmly against his body, and at the same time irritated that he should assume she had a blank diary and could come out with him at the drop of a hat. The annoying thing was, she thought ruefully, her evenings *were* mostly free, but since her afternoon with him at his cottage she had tried to keep out of his way. Her hungry response to his light kiss still sent a hot flush of embarrassment through her.

'I'll just go and change,' she said hastily, firmly extricating herself from Mike's arm. 'It'll be even more difficult to do this run if I wear this clobber!'

Nervously Lindy looked at the large crowd assembled by the starters' post. She was beginning to feel that she'd made a huge mistake, offering to take part. She really didn't think her body was up to it! Most of the other participants looked horribly fit and as if they did this sort of thing on a regular basis.

Mrs Fyles-Smith was stretching her muscles in a professional way, her body toned and bronzed from assiduous weight training and sun-bed treatment. She was surrounded by a group of laughing, loud-voiced people, casually dressed in designer gear, who'd obviously come to cheer her on.

A little boy with a baseball cap put on back to front was jumping up and down in front of Mike. Lindy could hear his excited little voice. 'I've been on the go-karts, Mike! I like them better than the bouncy castle—a boy fell on me there!'

He just had to be Max. He was a miniature carbon copy of his uncle—even from here Lindy could see the set of his nose and chin, the dark hair and wide blue eyes. Mike was pulling the child's hair affectionately.

'I'm just getting ready for the fun run now, Max. Why don't you go with your mum and have biscuits and drinks waiting for us at the finishing line?'

The little boy was off like an arrow, shouting over his shoulder, 'I'll get you biscuits, Mike—trillions of 'em!'

Lindy chuckled to herself—it didn't look as if Max had been too traumatised by events in his young life!

She watched as Mike stripped off his tracksuit and revealed a powerful body in running shorts and a brief singlet. She bit her lip—it wasn't fair that he looked so absolutely fabulous! As if he could feel her gaze on him, he looked up and waved at her, his eyes sweeping appreciatively over her tall figure. She smiled back weakly, his close scrutiny of her making her suddenly conscious of the amount of leg her shorts were revealing and the fact that her T-shirt fitted round her bust rather too snugly! Damn it—I look like an amateur, she thought crossly. Then she gazed at the rest of the field and relaxed slightly, noting that some of the older surgeons were taking part and a lot of them looked like she felt, unfit and slightly apprehensive!

The gun went off, and suddenly everyone was running, in rather a ragged, rabble-like way. Lindy found herself swept along with the crowd and tried to concentrate hard on keeping a steady pace, but most of all not going too quickly—she didn't want to collapse at the first corner! In fact, after a few minutes, when she'd settled into a steady rhythm, she began to quite enjoy the feeling of stretching her long legs and breathing air deep into her lungs. She could see Mike ahead of her, his tall figure easily striding at the head of the bunch. Firmly Lindy switched her eyes to a stout man just in front of her, puffing his way gamely along the track, clad in an unlikely combination of hospital greens and football boots.

The run was nearly halfway through and Lindy was beginning to feel that heaven would be a hot bath with a steaming cup of tea. Muscles she didn't know she possessed had started aching, and her feet screamed out for her to stop. It didn't help that Mike had dropped back to run beside her, smiling encouragingly, unaware of the pain barrier she was going through, making it difficult for her to smile back at him. No way did she want him to know that the whole exercise was becoming more than she'd bargained for!

'This is good fun, isn't it?' he commented, no hint of breathlessness in his voice. 'If the rain holds off we should be in quite soon. You're certainly coping well—enjoying it?'

'Yes,' gasped Lindy, her legs now moving on autopilot. 'Can't wait to do another one!'

A flicker of admiration in his eyes showed that Mike was more aware of her discomfort than she knew. 'That's the spirit,' he murmured. 'Have a drink at this next station—we mustn't get dehydrated.'

They slowed down and Lindy gratefully took sips of bottled water from one of the volunteers.

'Keep your legs moving,' advised Mike. 'You don't want to stiffen up. How do your calf muscles feel?'

'Fine!' Lindy smiled, bending down cautiously and trying to rub the agonising tightness out of them.

Mike looked down at her kindly. 'Allow me,' he murmured, bending down and massaging her calves firmly with his strong hands. He looked up at her, his eyes twinkling. 'Is that better?'

'Much better,' said Lindy faintly, wondering how much longer she could bear the exquisite feel of his powerful touch and hoping he would stop at her calf muscles!

She was hardly aware of the other joggers pounding past them. Suddenly there were just Mike and her, very close together, their scantily clad bodies tantalisingly close in their own little world. Even in the breathless state she was in, she was intensely conscious of his powerful frame next to hers, could smell the male smell of him. Another two inches and they would touch each other…

He gazed down at her intently. 'All right to continue? Take it slowly—we're nearly home. Just think of the meal I'm going to give you tonight—you'll be needing it!'

Mike certainly never gave up, thought Lindy wryly, taking another last gulp of water. 'I haven't said I can come yet,' she said briskly. 'I've got so much to do…'

Mike smiled enigmatically at her. 'You'll come!' he said airily. 'Anyway, I've booked a table! Now, let's get going—we don't want to get left behind. Are you up to it?'

Lindy flashed him a look of irritation. He seemed to assume that she would fall in with his plans automatically, and that he was doubtful that she could complete the run!

'Of course, I'm up to it,' she said brusquely. 'I'm raring to go!'

He looked at her, chuckling. 'Glad you like a challenge, Lindy!'

They set off again, their arms almost touching each other. Lindy's legs felt less painful, and she began to think she'd got her second wind. Running with Mike beside her was giving her confidence that she could finish the course.

*   *   *

The cloudburst came without any warning: one minute everyone was running under clear blue skies, then suddenly there was a clap of thunder and it seemed that a huge bucket of water had been tipped over the whole crowd. Lindy gasped as the cold rain hit her, and in no time at all people were slithering about in thick mud, shrieking as they got wet through. Lindy continued grimly on—she was certainly not going to give up in front of Mike. Why, she could see the finishing line, and it would be good to feel she'd achieved the whole thing!

In front of them the stout man dressed in hospital greens and looking rather laboured was beginning to slow down—they would pass him any minute. She felt quite proud of herself and shot a look at Mike under her lashes, wondering if he'd noticed how well she was doing. She would definitely take up jogging as a serious aid to fitness in the future!

Lindy noticed as they overtook the stout man that he had stopped and was bending over with his hands on his knees—probably trying to catch his breath, she thought sympathetically. Then, as she watched, he slowly toppled to the ground with a groan, his body falling into the mud with a sickening squelching sound.

With a gasp of shock, Lindy slithered to a halt, then ran back, sinking to her knees beside the sick runner. She was aware that Mike had dropped down beside her, and with his powerful arms was managing to turn the unfortunate man over, large though he was. The man was pulling at the tied ribbons of the hospital greens as though they were strangling him.

'Can't breathe,' he rasped gutturally. 'The pain's crushing me…'

Automatically she started to talk to him, soothing

words of comfort. 'You'll be all right. We're here to help you. Don't worry and don't try to talk.'

His face was chalky grey, his eyes wide with fear and pain, choking as he tried to take in breath. Lindy pulled the incongruous hospital greens he was wearing back from his chest, and laid two fingers on the side of his neck. His pulse was weak and fluttering. Lindy guessed he was having a major heart attack.

Many of the sliding figures round her had drawn up to help, but Mike waved them on as he stabbed out numbers on his mobile phone. It was better not to have too many anxious people crowding the patient.

'It's OK,' he murmured to a nurse who was part of the fun run and who'd also come up to help. 'Sister Jenkins is here, and a blue-light ambulance is on its way. We'll soon have this gentleman in safe hands.'

Lindy searched round for something to prop the man up and help him breathe more easily, grabbing a fleece someone handed to her and pushing it in a roll behind the patient's back. She felt a wave of relief that someone as competent and experienced as Mike should be on hand in this emergency because, although there were St John Ambulance volunteers dotted about the course, and many medics actually running, immediate medical response in this sort of crisis was of paramount importance.

Almost immediately, the siren of the ambulance could be heard above the lashing rain as it raced across the grass of the park. Even as it drove up to them, the man began choking and his face turned deep purple.

'Get an airway in p.d.q.,' shouted Mike above the noise of the worsening weather to the paramedic who leapt down from the vehicle. 'He's arresting!'

Lindy moved away from the patient so that the plastic airway could be inserted into his mouth and grabbed the cardiac box handed to her, filled with life-support pre-packed injectible drugs. The paramedic had pinched the man's nostrils shut and was blowing sharply into the airway, watching his chest after every puff to see if the patient's lungs were inflating.

Lindy handed Mike a stethoscope from the box and he put it on the man's chest, listening intently to the labouring heart.

'We need shots of adrenaline and atropine,' he murmured, holding his hand out for the appropriate syringe. 'We'll try and settle the rhythm.'

He monitored the man's heart again after the drugs had been administered, and eventually nodded to the ambulance crew, leaning back on his heels. 'OK. It's reasonably stable now. Get him to CCU.'

Lindy puffed her cheeks out with relief as she watched the ambulance make its way slowly up the slope again. Her own heart was thudding with the shock of seeing someone dropping to the ground in front of her. She might be a casualty nurse, but it wasn't quite what she'd expected on a fun run!

'I hope the poor man makes it,' she murmured.

'If he doesn't get pneumonia from being soaked to the skin, he has every chance. He couldn't have been nearer the hospital,' observed Mike. He gave an amused glance down at Lindy sitting on the water-logged ground, her hair plastered to her head and rivulets of water cascading down her face.

'I think it's time we headed for shelter now,' he suggested wryly. He put out his hand and pulled her up by her arms. 'When you're warm and dry, I'll take you to this little country pub I know that does delicious soups and hotpots—I think you deserve it.'

She looked at him nervously through the lashing rain. He looked as if he were standing under a shower, but his blue eyes shone through, twinkling wickedly at her. The thought of hot soup sounded terribly tempting—then she remembered the empty fridge at her house, and the load of shopping she'd intended to do after the fun run, not to mention a rapid clean-up all round and a week's pile of ironing! Sheila and some girlfriends were coming for lunch the next day, and she had nothing to offer them at the moment except some stale cheese and bread. She was glad of a truthful excuse to get her out of being alone with Mike—however tempting the meal sounded. Even more, perhaps she wanted to demonstrate her own independence when it came to accepting invitations—she didn't want him to think she was at his beck and call after her behaviour at his cottage!

'It's impossible,' she said firmly. 'I'm too busy and I have things to do this evening.'

'Nothing's impossible,' he said equally firmly. 'Come on, let's get going.'

He set off at a great pace up the hill and Lindy sighed. She'd have it out with him later, she decided, as she plodded wearily after him. Meanwhile, she began to revise her thoughts about taking up jogging as a regular pursuit—perhaps it wasn't such an attractive activity after all!

Oh, the blissfulness of the hot cup of chocolate laced liberally with whisky that Jane pressed into her hand!

'Get that into you,' Jane said gruffly. 'Purely medicinal and to get your body temperature up! I might have known there'd be some emergency along the line with that fun run!' There was a slight hint of satisfaction in her voice that she'd been proved right after all!

Lindy sat swathed in a hospital gown and blanket in the kitchen of Casualty after a needle-sharp hot shower. The other fun-runners seemed to have melted out of sight, and she stretched her limbs out luxuriously, feeling the hot liquid form a comforting trail down her gullet.

'That,' she said gratefully to Janet, 'is just what I needed! What happened to the heart patient they brought in?'

'He's in CCU and it's touch and go, I believe. What an unfit man of over sixty thinks he doing on a run, I don't know. He's probably not attempted such sustained exercise for years,' observed Janet tartly as she stumped off to get updates on some other casualties of the afternoon.

Lindy leant back against the chair and closed her eyes—she could go to sleep for a thousand years after her exertions during the past few hours! She would get ready and creep out to do her shopping and go home before Mike pounced on her for this meal he'd mentioned. He had disappeared to get dry and change, but she was *not* going to risk being alone with him again for a long time!

The supermarket had been crowded and full of irritable people doing a late Saturday afternoon shop with broods of noisy children. Now Lindy sank gratefully onto a kitchen chair, dumping her loaded plastic bags onto the table. She felt as if she'd taken part in a great battle. She looked round at the little kitchen despondently, and saw a letter which had arrived that morning. She would look at it later, she decided, stuffing it into her handbag. First she would force herself to have a mammoth clean and put the ton of shopping away. She got up and opened the fridge door. Miraculously an unopened bottle of wine was on the bottom shelf—a glass or two would be just the thing to kick-start her into her busy evening!

She wandered into the bedroom with a refreshing glass, taking a large mouthful, and with renewed vigour started folding the jumpers she seemed to have abandoned on the floor during the week, putting them back in drawers. Then, encouraged by the look of the bedroom, she worked with lightning speed on dispersing the shopping in the kitchen, flicking a damp cloth over the work surfaces and plonking a small bunch of daffodils into a vase on the table. She stood back and looked with satisfaction at her handiwork—it didn't take long to make her little flat look habitable.

The sudden piercing sound of the front doorbell made her jump, then she smiled. The young couple next door were always running out of something. Last night it had been sugar, tonight it was probably milk.

Lindy opened the door with a welcoming smile, which died on her lips as she saw who the visitor was. Mike was standing on the doorstep, looking anything but pleased and quite different from his normal relaxed attitude! His face glowered as he looked at her with angry blue eyes.

'Where the hell did you disappear to? I've been looking for you for ages! I was beginning to think something had happened to you.'

'What do you mean? The run was over, I was tired and I came home!' She looked crossly at him. Talk about making assumptions! 'I told you I had plans of my own this evening,' she said loftily, feeling a crazy mixture of excitement at his presence and resentment at his presumption.

Mike folded his arms. 'You agreed to go out for a meal with me when we'd finished today. I didn't expect you to go running off!'

Lindy flushed. Echoes of the power Jake used to have over her sprang into her mind. 'I didn't agree to anything,' she snapped. 'I said I had a lot to do. You don't own me!'

She started to shut the door firmly, but Mike put up his hand and held it open, looking more conciliatory. 'Perhaps I've been a little premature, but you did say you'd allow me to make it up to you…'

Lindy sighed and felt herself weakening. He was certainly persistent! 'Oh, you'd better come in,' she said at last, too weary to argue for long. 'But, I warn you, I'm dead on my feet after today's effort!'

'That's why I thought a hot meal at this pub would be a good idea,' he said. He followed her through the little flat to the kitchen, and sat on a chair at the table, his long legs spread out in front of him, watching her for a minute. His eyes roved slowly over her from her glossy hair down to her long-legged statuesque figure.

'You know, you're going to have to stop this,' he said finally.

'Stop what?' Lindy looked at him, mystified.

'Running away. I don't know what you're frightened of, Lindy, but I'm not an ogre, you know. I'm not going to hurt you.'

Colour rose in her face and she tilted her chin defiantly at him. 'I'm not frightened of anything, Mike Corrigan. Perhaps I'm merely being careful—careful who I choose to be friends with.'

He got up and stepped towards her, putting his hands

on her shoulders. 'Rubbish! There's something holding you back—it's not being careful, it's being inhibited!'

'How dare you?' Lindy stared at him, her deep brown eyes flashing angrily in rage. 'Please, don't make assumptions about me—you know nothing about me or why I'm like I am.'

He smiled, a gentle, kindly smile, and shook his head. 'I don't make assumptions—I'm trying not to guess. But, Lindy…' His hands tightened on her shoulders. 'The other week when you were at the cottage, there was something between us there—a spark of attraction, something… Call it what you will, but you fancied me, Lindy Jenkins! You've been avoiding me since then and I want to know what I've done wrong.'

She swallowed, stopping in the full flow of her anger and flushing as the memory of that afternoon washed over her in equal measures of embarrassment and shame. Of course she was frightened of involving herself with someone else…perhaps she'd never be able to trust another man again. Nevertheless she'd led him on then, and she couldn't tell him yet why she'd backed away so peremptorily.

'We learn by our mistakes,' she said at last. 'I didn't want a repeat of things that have happened to me in the past. I was wrong to give you the impression that I was…available. I shouldn't have done that. We've only just met each other and it was stupid of me to…respond to you like I did.'

He grinned and put his hands up as if in surrender. 'Enough said. We've all had a learning curve to go through from experience, and perhaps I'm being a mite sensitive. Let's forget about the whole thing, just be friends! Now, what about this lovely hot meal that's going to do us good?'

His apparent acceptance of the situation suddenly made the atmosphere lift, and Lindy felt herself relax with relief. Impulsively she reached into the fridge and held the wine up. It had been a long day, and perhaps it would be nice to eat something someone else had cooked after all.

'How about a glass?' she offered, then gave an impish smile. 'Before we go out?'

CHAPTER SIX

IN THE dark cosiness of the little pub, with its soft golden lighting and cheery fire, Lindy suddenly thought what a good idea it had been after all to go out that evening. Just driving out into the countryside around Manorfield had been enough to relax her after the busy week she'd had at the hospital, followed by the fun run. She wondered why on earth didn't she do it more often—she seemed to have been stuck in the confines of the town for ages. Jake's notion of a night out had been a sophisticated club where he'd be likely to meet the 'right' people, and casual comfortable dress had not been an option.

Coming out here brought back to her how beautiful the scenery was—the ancient forest with its mist of fresh green that spread along the lower slopes of the hills, and the moorland beyond, just beginning to show the faintest purple from the heather. Gradually she felt the tensions of work slipping from her shoulders, and she leant back in her chair with a faint smile on her lips.

She watched Mike as he wove his way back to their table with drinks. His tall, broad figure and striking dark looks were attracting attention from most of the women in the room, she thought with amusement. He seemed oblivious of the notice they were giving him as he carefully put down her drink.

'What have you chosen to eat?' he asked. 'I'm starving—I need an injection of energy after that fun run!'

'You've had quite a full day,' remarked Lindy, taking a refreshing draught of the chilled spritzer she'd ordered. 'I hope we've made lots of money.'

He sat down opposite her and nodded. 'Yes, it would be a tragedy if the hospital had to close—let's hope it doesn't happen. I don't want to lose my job there— especially as I'm getting to know such congenial colleagues.' His eyes smiled across at her, and she felt an answering blush. 'Now,' he added briskly, 'I can recommend one pumpkin and orange soup followed by the hotpot—both wonderfully warm and refreshing. You'll feel you could do the fun run all over again when you've eaten that!'

'You've got to be joking,' Lindy giggled, the combined effects of the wine from home and the spritzer she'd ordered beginning to kick in. 'It's going to take me *weeks* to recover from this afternoon's torture! The food sounds good, though—I'll go for that!'

Mike smiled at her, noting the fresh blush on her cheeks, the way her lashes fanned onto her high cheekbones when she looked down and that sensual full mouth, just needing to be kissed and caressed by his— when the time was right. He'd nearly blown his chances this afternoon, pushing her into a corner by getting her to admit she fancied him! Now she looked so relaxed, leaning back in her chair and lifting her face to laugh up at him. Her long, slim young neck with its delicious little hollow led tantalisingly to the swell of her breasts beneath the dark blue silk blouse she was wearing. He gritted his teeth. She was absolutely gorgeous, but he had to be patient or he'd never find out about that something in her past which, he suspected, coloured her present so much.

Lindy was laughing at him. 'Wake up, daydreamer,'

she murmured. 'Our food's here. I thought you said you were starving!'

The soup smelt delicious and came with large wedges of warm home-baked brown bread. Lindy fell on it as if she hadn't seen food before, grinning rather shamefacedly at Mike as she mopped up the last vestiges with a crust.

'First food I've had all day,' she explained through a mouthful of bread. 'I don't normally eat this much!'

'Then you should,' Mike replied, his eyes twinkling at the enthusiasm with which she'd tackled the food. 'There was a department in the hospital in New York which dealt solely with girls and some boys who had eating disorders. Life had become a joyless thing, revolving funnily enough around food—and how to escape from eating it.'

Lindy put her head on one side and screwed up her eyes at Mike as if assessing him. 'What made you want to be a doctor, Mike? Did you come from a medical family?'

He laughed, throwing back his head and showing his strong white teeth. 'The very opposite.' He grinned. 'My parents hated anything to do with doctors—my mother was frightened of them, and my father distrusted them because they were always trying to make him give up his drinking. To no avail, I might add.'

'They must have been very proud of you, though,' Lindy persisted.

Mike's expression changed slightly, a look of sadness tinging his blue eyes. 'I guess my mother was pleased when I told her I wanted to do medicine, although she didn't live long enough to see me qualify. My father had disappeared long before I'd decided what I wanted to do.'

'So what inspired you? Television? Books?'

'No,' he said, looking into the distance as if recalling the moment. 'None of those. It was the reality of being involved in an accident when I was a little boy, and seeing a young doctor cope with it, and how he made the people round him feel—calming the panic and helping the victim. I was very impressed by that. It seemed such a worthwhile thing to do, to help frightened people in a practical way. I've never regretted it.'

Suddenly Lindy felt a wave of admiration for him. Mike hadn't said as much, but life had obviously been a battle. One didn't become a doctor without hard work and dedication, and usually the backing of one's parents—and it sounded as if he hadn't had much of the latter. She thought of her own mother—not the one who'd given birth to her, but the cheery, comfortable woman who had brought her up so lovingly, lavishing affection on her and giving her every support when she'd said she'd wanted to be a nurse—just like she had been. There were some things Lindy had to be very thankful for.

'Penny for them,' said Mike with a smile. He had been watching her intently. 'What were you thinking about?'

'My mother,' said Lindy simply. 'She was a star. Looked after my father full time as he'd been crippled after a fall, but she'd been a nurse so that helped. She was really thrilled that I was following in her footsteps.'

'It must have been handed down in the genes,' remarked Mike.

Lindy gave a funny little laugh. 'I don't know about that!' She paused for a moment, toying with her knife and fork. 'It would be interesting to know,' she said slowly, 'just what I did have handed down in my genes!'

'Have you any brothers or sisters?' Mike asked with interest.

'No, I guess I was enough for them! I would have liked that,' she said wistfully, 'because both my parents died—my father some time ago, my mother only last year—and now I've no one really to share my memories of them with. They gave me a very happy childhood.'

Lindy applied herself with enthusiasm to the next course, a steaming hotpot with dark rich gravy and meat that fell apart when you touched it. She couldn't remember enjoying a meal so much for years. It seemed almost comical to think back to the pathetic meals she'd had with Jake, pushing a salad leaf around a plate when she'd been longing to have a thick steak because she'd known he disapproved of women wolfing down man-sized meals! She must have been mad, she decided, finishing her final mouthful with satisfaction. She was beginning to realise just how much she'd allowed Jake to dominate her life.

She leaned back with a sigh of contentment. 'That,' she said happily, 'was absolutely delicious. I couldn't eat another thing!'

Mike raised one sardonic eyebrow at her. 'Oh, come,' he protested. 'Surely a little bit of bread-and-butter pudding, or a slice of Bakewell tart?'

'Not for me,' declared Lindy, standing up. 'I'm just going to the ladies—but you have something to fill the corners.'

As she left the table, her bag swung open and a letter dropped out. Mike bent down and picked it up, placing it by her plate. His eye caught the address as he put it down, and he took another, closer look at it with interest.

'This letter dropped from your handbag,' he said to Lindy when she returned.

'Ah, yes, thank you. I forgot about that. I put it in my bag this afternoon to read later.'

'I couldn't help seeing that it was addressed to Madeline Jenkins—I didn't realise Lindy was a shortened form of Madeline,' he remarked. 'It's quite unusual—why don't you call yourself that now? I like it.'

Lindy shrugged. 'There was another girl in the nursing school called Madeline, and it got a bit confusing. Everyone started to call me Lindy, and it sort of stuck. It was strange at first as I'd always been called Madeline since I was little—my mother used to call me that.'

'Madeline,' Mike repeated slowly. 'Yes, the name suits you. For some reason I always think of a Madeline as someone with your dark, sherry-coloured eyes—did you know they have golden lights in them when you laugh?'

Lindy chuckled. 'Now you're being fanciful—I'm glad I've got good eyesight, that's all!'

'What about coffee?' Mike suggested.

Lindy shook her head. 'I'm so full at the moment—perhaps a little later. We could,' she said brightly, 'have coffee at the flat if you want…'

It had to be the wine talking, she thought ruefully as soon as she'd said it. She'd warned herself not to be alone with Mike Corrigan for a long, long time! And now, a week or so after she'd pledged to keep away from him, here she was, extending invitations back to the flat! The unaccustomed alcohol had given her that devil-may-care feeling, however, and what harm could a little cup of coffee do?

Lindy went into the kitchen and put some coffee into the filter machine. She'd managed to find some brandy hidden at the back of a cupboard and had poured them each a generous tumblerful. Now Mike was sprawled in front of the television in the other room, watching the highlights of a football match. He'd rung up for a taxi to come in half an hour as obviously he couldn't enjoy the brandy and drive.

It had been an unexpectedly happy evening, Lindy reflected as she poured boiling water onto the coffee grounds, relaxed and easy. She sipped the brandy as she considered all the things they'd talked about. She'd learned more about Mike that evening than she had from the few weeks he'd worked with her. From his revelations of how he'd become a doctor she guessed he was a man of grit and determination, not to be deflected from his aims.

She could just imagine him as a little boy, watching the doctor at the scene of the accident and being fascinated and impressed by the man. She remembered being taken to an exhibition tennis match when she was young—how she'd longed and longed to become a wonderful player like the graceful people on the court. She had reached quite a reasonable standard, but the old injury to her arm all those years ago had weakened it, preventing her from ever aspiring to top-class play.

She shrugged to herself—she'd moved on from there. Her arm never bothered her now, and the ugly scar had become part of her—a little marker in her life.

'That coffee smells fantastic!'

Lindy whipped round. Mike was close behind her,

leaning against the doorjamb. His eyes crinkled up with amusement at her startled reaction.

'Sorry, I didn't mean to startle you—can I help?'

Lindy breathed a little faster. She was so close to those deep blue eyes, the wide mobile mouth and his dark thick hair—a little nearer and they would be touching, hip to hip, breast to breast. Was it the brandy or a dart of desire that caused her stomach to flutter and her heart to hammer against her ribs? She gulped and held fast to the back of a chair, flicking a glance at his expression, wondering if he was feeling the same way, too.

'No...no, I'm don't need any help.' Her voice sounded slightly strained. 'It...it was a lovely meal,' she added falteringly.

'It was a wonderful evening,' he replied softly.

For a second they were silent and as still as statues, staring at each other as if their eyes were locked. Then slowly but inexorably he moved towards her, and his arms pulled her gently but firmly against him. His mouth was on hers, setting her lips on fire, and they melted together in a long and passionate kiss that seemed to last for ever. His mouth was gentle but demanding, teasing open her lips, exploring her greedily.

'My God, Lindy—you're so incredibly beautiful,' he whispered, moving his lips down to that delectable hollow in her neck and nibbling the soft skin there with sensual butterfly kisses.

Lindy felt she was drowning. It was as if she'd suddenly fallen into a sea of abandoned passion, with delicious sensations trailing like tiny electric currents through her body, and a maelstrom of emotions were whirling round in her head.

She was faintly aware of a little voice whispering to

her that she shouldn't be doing this. Hadn't it only been a few hours ago that she'd apologised for leading Mike on that afternoon at his cottage? But the brandy and wine, mixed with the incredible sexual attraction she felt for him, seemed to make all the inhibitions she'd had before float away like seeds in the wind.

She tried to push that insistent voice out of her mind. For that second she no longer cared what she did—she wanted to live for the moment. She wound her arms round Mike's neck and pressed herself against his hard chest, allowing him to do what he wanted with his hands and lips.

'Don't stop,' she murmured. 'This is lovely.'

He smiled down at her tenderly, his hand cupping her breast gently. 'And this is exquisite…'

His lips were trailing down to the satin skin of her cleavage, his body hard and demanding against hers. He wanted her as much as she did him, and she arched against him, feeling his need, ignoring that irritating voice in her head. Then abruptly, and almost shockingly, she felt him draw away from her, holding her gently at arm's length.

He looked down at her quizzically, but there was a burning look of desire in his eyes, and his hands tightened convulsively on her shoulders.

'And I thought you only wanted to be friends,' he joked softly, a catch in his voice. 'Do you think, after what you said, that perhaps we're getting *too* friendly? I don't want you to regret this!'

Lindy stared at him, bewildered for a second at his withdrawal, then jolted into cold reality. Thank God he'd reminded her and given her the chance to pull herself together before they both did something they'd rue later on.

'Sorry!' she said, forcing a light tone into her voice and smiling brightly. 'Shouldn't have had quite so much of the vino—went to my head slightly!'

Shakily she pulled her silk blouse straight and dashed her hair from her eyes. It had been such a wonderful few minutes, an insight as to just how marvellous it would be to be made love to by Mike—but not yet, not yet. She would be doing it for all the wrong reasons probably—low self-esteem after her break-up with Jake, the need to be desired by a man again... It wouldn't be fair on either of them.

The sudden strident ring of the doorbell startled them both, and Mike looked wryly down at her.

'I'd forgotten about the taxi.' He grimaced. He picked up his glass and finished the brandy in one gulp. Then he bent down to brush her lips with his.

'To friendship,' he said softly. 'May it grow deeper and stronger every day!'

Lindy stared at him wordlessly, her heart thumping wildly against her ribs. She wanted to shout at him to stay, to hold her—in a friendly way—and talk to her about friendship, and how it might turn to love someday, but she couldn't.

His eyes lost their sombre look, and twinkled wickedly at her. 'I don't want us to make love because we've both had a bit of alcohol—I want you to fancy me when you're stone-cold sober as well!'

Then he bent over her for a second, stroking her face, and said very seriously, 'Friendship's a wonderful thing, isn't it? It'll be fun getting to know each other.'

After he had gone, Lindy lay on her bed, an unexpected happiness filling her completely for the first time in weeks. So, she'd had some wine and so had he, but that had just relaxed them, and this 'friendship' thing he'd talked about hadn't sounded at all dull or sterile. It had sounded... She searched for the word. Yes, it had sounded fun and exciting and possibly the prelude to something more profound! If Mike wanted to take things slowly, not force the pace, then so did she. It made a refreshing change in her experience, she thought wryly, for a man to want to hold something back. It was tantalising and beguiling, and she couldn't wait to see him again!

She reflected that friendship had meant nothing to Jake. She was beginning to realise she'd fallen for a shell—someone with tremendous power and influence on the outside, capable of charm, but ruthless on the inside, determined to get his own way whether it hurt anybody or not. He had deceived her and shattered her confidence, and Lindy supposed that that was what had made it so hard to give herself easily again. Now she felt as if her heart had been set free after a long imprisonment.

Singing softly to herself, she wandered back into the kitchen and washed the glasses and cups, then picked up the handbag on the table. The letter was still poking out of the top. She opened it with a knife and read the contents closely. Then she sat down rather suddenly and read it carefully again. Her hands trembled as she finished it and put it back in the envelope.

It had arrived! At long last she had the information she'd been waiting for over the past few months. Her heart raced uncomfortably and her mouth felt dry— suddenly the way was open for her to find out about her past, and she wasn't sure if she had the courage to do it. She sat for a long time, gazing blankly at the wall in front of her.

* * *

Following her unexpectedly happy evening with Mike, Lindy started on night duty—and somehow even that didn't seem a chore at the moment, she thought light-heartedly a few days later as she jotted down information on the whiteboard. She could put up with any-thing—Janet's short fuse, even Jack's disappearances when she needed him most. Just to know Mike was somewhere in the building sent her metabolic rate soar-ing, and she got through her paperwork in half the time she had before. Yes, they were just friends, but she had that excited feeling that it might turn to more than that, given time. She could wait...

Lindy stopped writing on the board for a second and sighed. Everything should have been utterly wonder-ful—and yet she had a niggling little worry at the back of her mind to do with the letter she'd received. It was the key to finding out about her past, which she longed to do—but would she be doing the right thing by turn-ing that key, or making one of the biggest mistakes in her life? Perhaps it was a risk she had to take. She bit her lip, frowning thoughtfully at the board she'd been writing on. This was something she wanted to keep to herself for a while.

Her worried reverie was interrupted by Carrie's soft Irish lilt. 'A man with stab wounds has just come in, Sister. Dr Corrigan's with him at the moment, but he wants some assistance.' The young student nurse gave a little giggle. 'It's really funny—you should just see the patient!'

Lindy raised an eyebrow rather disapprovingly at the young student nurse. 'I wouldn't have thought a stab wound is much fun, Nurse. Perhaps you could go and check the emergency trays for me while I see what's happened.'

Lindy swept off down the corridor and chuckled inwardly to herself. Carrie was a bit zany and had to be reproved at times for totally inappropriate remarks, but her heart was in the right place. She went into the emergency room, wondering just what it was that had amused Carrie so much.

A grossly overweight man with a shaven head was lying on his stomach, a towel spread over his lower body. Across his back were several stab wounds, some of which were bleeding quite profusely. From the strong smell of alcohol that permeated the room, Lindy guessed that the patient had had a boozy night—people tended to bleed more freely when they had alcohol in their blood.

Mike had his stethoscope on the man's back, trying to listen to his lungs and ascertain if they'd been penetrated by the knife wound.

'This is Mr Ian Hedges,' he informed Lindy, looking quizzically at her over the dangling stethoscope. 'Apparently he had an altercation with some youths outside a nightclub. I'm just trying to hear if he's damaged his lungs, but the breath sounds are normal. There seems quite a lot of blood loss. Can you put up a drip, and cross-match two units, please? He may need a transfusion.'

Ian Hedges groaned and said thickly, 'I'll swing for those bastards—they didn't give me a chance to give them one back. And those bloody police! They manhandled me—that's what they did! I'll damn well sue them!'

'Never mind, Mr Hedges,' soothed Lindy, pulling on latex gloves before she swabbed the wounds and mopped up some of the blood. 'Just lie still and let Dr Corrigan inspect these wounds.'

She put a blood-pressure monitor on his arm. 'Not too bad. He's maintaining BP at 110/70—slight reflex tachycardia,' she murmured.

'I think you've been lucky, Mr Hedges,' remarked Mike, stuffing his stethoscope back in his pocket. 'These wounds look worse than they are—I don't think you've damaged anything too vital. None of them are very deep. We'll be able to patch you up all right.'

'Glad you think I've been lucky,' grunted the man. 'It was my stag night and I'm due to get married in the morning—what's my flaming bride going to say if I don't turn up?'

Lindy pulled back the towel and a dressing that had been covering a wound on his lower back. Across each buttock was tattooed the legend LOVE ME STUPID! surrounded by graphics of hearts and flowers.

'How romantic!' murmured Mike, looking gravely down at the wounded groom. His laughing eyes flicked up to meet Lindy's in mutual hilarity. 'We'll do our best to get you ready for your blushing bride, Mr Hedges!'

No wonder Carrie was amused, thought Lindy with an inward chuckle.

In the little kitchen, Mike poured himself a strong coffee and grinned across at Lindy. 'Well, that was one of the lighter moments in a pretty fraught night! I'd never thought of having a tattoo on my rear end, but some people must find it attractive!'

Lindy giggled. 'He certainly wouldn't turn me on— perhaps his fiancée is made of sterner stuff than I am!'

'I don't know about that.' Mike's eyes twinkled in amusement. 'You showed you had plenty of mettle during the fun run!' He put down his cup. 'Which reminds me, we've got to get our act together for the next fund-raising event in a few weeks—the Midsummer Ball. There's quite a lot to sort out, so there's a meeting tomorrow night at my cottage. We'll have finished night duty then, so you will be there, won't you?'

A short while ago Lindy might have felt too drained to contemplate helping out even at a picnic party. With her new-found optimism she felt quite excited at the idea.

He went on smoothly, 'As we're organising the thing together, I take it you'll be coming to the ball with me as my partner—unless there's someone else you've got in mind? I think you'll like the crowd I'm getting together.'

Suddenly, instead of the thrill she should have felt at the invitation, a shiver of foreboding darted through her. All at once Mike's words had a very distinct echo of Jake's authoritarian tones—the assumption that she would automatically agree to be his partner, going with a group of *his* friends. Mike had a tendency to assume things, she reflected, but was she being a mite over-sensitive?

She frowned and was silent for a minute, biting her lip. Then she said quickly, 'Please, don't think you have to take me just because we're on the same committee—there's always someone around I can ask.'

'I can believe that,' said Mike quietly. His blue eyes looked at her thoughtfully. 'I'd really like you to come with me, you know. Not just because we're organising it but because, well, we *are* friends, aren't we?'

She pulled a strand of hair behind her ears and looked down, embarrassed. Of course she'd like to go with him, but that wary feeling of being taken over, almost 'owned', by a man still lingered at the back of her mind.

Mike stepped forward and folded his arms in front of her, a spark of anger in his blue eyes. 'You're back-tracking again, aren't you?' Suddenly his tone was impatient, accusing. 'For heaven's sake, what's the problem? Maybe I'm being too inquisitive, but I have a feeling that something went drastically wrong between you and your last boyfriend! There *was* a boyfriend, wasn't there—am I right?'

Lindy stared at him in shock at the unexpected question—how on earth did he know about Jake?

'W-what do you mean?' she stuttered, 'What boyfriend?'

'Oh, come on, Lindy, it stands out a mile. It doesn't take a genius to work out you've been hurt, and you don't believe anyone can care for you again! I've noticed it before—this fear of giving yourself. As soon as I get a little closer to you, I get rebuffed. Seems to me that's because someone's made you lose your confidence. All I've done is ask you to come to a dance with me, but you're frightened to accept, aren't you?'

She flushed and tilted her chin rather defiantly at him. Was she that transparent?

'To be honest,' she said in a clipped tone, 'you didn't *ask* me to the dance, you *told* me I was going with you—there's a difference, you know.'

He laughed. 'So that's it! I'm taking you for granted, am I? Come on, sweetheart, loosen up! Don't let this ex of yours make you over-sensitive!'

Perhaps he was right and she was getting things out of proportion, but a mere few weeks ago she'd been thrown on the scrap heap. Her mouth compressed. She couldn't help it, but it rankled slightly that he should think she was making a fuss about nothing. Jake had been her whole life for many months—Mike could have no idea how that had affected her.

Lindy looked at him under her lashes. Should she tell Mike how foolish she'd been, how naïve to have been taken in by a smoothie like Jake? He would probably think she was a complete idiot to have been duped like she had.

For a second or two she was silent, then at last she said slowly, 'Yes, you're right. I did have a boyfriend—quite recently, in fact. We split up because he was…deceitful. He didn't really care who he hurt as long as he got his way.'

'Sounds charming,' observed Mike drily, watching her flushed face and troubled eyes. 'What made you fall for him, then?'

What indeed? she pondered. She gave a short laugh. 'Because he was powerful, generous when he wanted to be, and he introduced me to a glamorous, exciting life I'd never known before.' She sighed. 'Sounds shallow of me, I know, but I'd led a very sheltered, humdrum life before, and when my mother died, well, Jake stepped in and seemed to offer me things that were missing in my life—he dazzled me.'

'So what triggered the break-up?'

Lindy pressed her lips together—to tell him that would be a step too far at the moment. It was still an almost physical pain to think of how they'd broken up. The full horror of his betrayal could still make her mouth dry up and her heart hammer against her ribs, and to her embarrassment she felt two tears roll slowly down her cheeks.

Mike sprang forward with a horrified intake of breath, and put his arms round her protectively. 'For-

give me,' he murmured, putting his cheek against hers.
'I've blundered in where I shouldn't have. It's none of
my business—except that anything that hurts you
makes me angry…'

Lindy felt the comforting thud of his heart against
her breast, the soothing strength of his arms around her.
He was like a rock, a haven of security, and gradually
she felt herself relax.

His finger tilted her face towards his. 'I'm afraid I've
always been a bit impulsive,' he said ruefully. 'I jump
in before I've thought things out. I'm sorry—but the
man who hurt you must be a complete rat.'

'Don't be.' She sighed, 'What happened between
Jake and me was my fault—I should have been more
aware…'

'I don't believe that.' Mike's eyes raked over her
heart-shaped face and her warm, dark eyes turned up
to his. 'You're just too sweet and kind, I suspect. Your
first instinct is to trust people.'

His lips came down on hers, brushing them gently,
and he folded her against him again, patting her back
as one would to soothe a child. 'You must learn to
forget about the past…'

She looked up at him, slightly embarrassed about the
revelations she'd made and the intimate atmosphere
that seemed to have developed between them. She'd
wanted to keep the mess she'd made of her romantic
life to herself, and suddenly she'd blurted it out to a
man she'd only known a few weeks! It was almost a
relief when the sudden shrill sound of his bleeper made
him step back, reaching into his pocket to turn it off.

Mike gave a wry chuckle. 'Blast, you made me forget I'm on night duty at St Luke's!' He smiled ruefully
at her. 'I'll hope to see you later. Don't forget the meet-

ing tomorrow night—and don't forget,' he added softly, picking up the wall phone, 'that I'd like you to be my partner for the ball—if you want to come with me!'

Lindy smiled faintly. It was hard to tread the fine line between being too trusting and learning to believe in someone again.

CHAPTER SEVEN

LINDY picked up the post from the hallway and threw her bag wearily onto the table. How lovely to think that she'd come to the end of the night-shift stint for a while! The flickering light on the answerphone showed there was a message, and she pressed the rewind button waiting for the recorded voice. All she longed to do was soak in a hot bath and then fall into bed for a few hours. If it was the hospital to say there was an emergency she didn't think she could possibly gather the strength to go back and work!

As she waited for the answerphone to reach the message, her mind flicked to the heart-to-heart she'd had with Mike the previous day. Perhaps she'd have been better to keep her revelations about her romance with Jake to herself. She'd probably come over as a real wimp, content to let a selfish man dictate to her! She was glad there would be plenty of people around tonight at the meeting—she didn't feel like another tête-à-tête with Mike so soon. It was a little too disturbing, seeming to force comparisons between him and Jake.

Lindy lay back on the sofa, listening as the machine whirred to the beginning of the tape and a woman's voice started speaking. Then suddenly she was sitting bolt upright, her mouth dry and her heart starting to pound. Lindy had never heard the voice before, and yet as soon as she heard it she could guess who it was.

'A message for Madeline Jenkins,' said the warm, measured tones in a pleasant low voice. There was just

121

a hint of hesitation in the words. 'This is Angela Lovatt. Thank you for your letter and suggested date of meeting. That will be fine—I look forward to seeing you next week at Apsley Grange.'

There was a click and the message ended. Lindy stared at the telephone as if it were alive, then shakily rewound the machine to hear the message again, her heart thudding. She took a deep breath. There was no going back now—she would have to meet Angela Lovatt!

Lindy had thought she'd never get to sleep from excitement and nerves after that phone call, but after six hours she woke up feeling surprisingly refreshed and full of energy. It was a lovely late May afternoon—one of those days that gave clear skies and a slightly sharp tang to the air. Having spent ten days hardly putting her nose outside, Lindy decided the prospect of stretching her legs and walking to Mike's for the meeting was irresistible—it would only take about half an hour through the fields on the outskirts of Manorfield. She could always get a lift back with one of the others if it became too dark. She made herself an invigorating cup of tea, and then set out.

It felt wonderful to have some time to herself and think over the things that had happened to her lately. It was hard to believe that she could feel so positive and excited about life when a short time ago she'd been in despair. And it wasn't just because of Mike, she reflected, that life had changed. In a few days she'd know about her background, where she'd really come from—scary, but thrilling as well. Perhaps it would be a disastrous mistake, but she knew she'd regret it to the end of her life if she didn't follow it up. One thing she did know—it was something she would keep to herself for a while.

Mike's cottage looked wonderful, bathed in the early evening light, and she could see him in the garden, mowing the lawn with an old hand push-mower. He was dressed in faded khaki shorts and his chest was tanned and bare—and muscled like Mr Universe, Lindy noted with an amused grin. She glanced at her watch and frowned. She'd have thought most of the committee would have been there by now. It was nearly seven o'clock but she seemed to have been the first to arrive. She leant over the garden gate and waited until he turned towards her with the mower.

'Hello, there!' He strode over to her, looking slightly guilty. 'Been trying to get you on the phone—I didn't realise you'd be walking here. The meeting's been cancelled as several people have had to go on some evening course.' His eyes swept over her long-legged body in a crisp check cotton shirt and figure-hugging pedal-pushers, and he grinned cheekily. 'I'm glad I couldn't contact you. Now you're here we can have a pleasant evening together!'

Alone with Mike again so soon! Not quite what she'd intended. Lindy looked at him, slightly taken aback.

'No...no, I'll walk back home, it doesn't matter. Anyway, you're doing the lawn.'

An intimate evening alone with Mike had not been on her agenda. After her last conversation with him about the ball and her broken romance she felt a little time apart would be a good thing. She'd been expecting, and looking forward to, an informal, pleasant evening with her colleagues.

He looked at her sternly. 'You're here now, and I

shall be very affronted if you walk off again.' He opened the gate and drew her firmly into the garden. 'Look,' he said persuasively, 'we'll have a glass of wine and a stroll by the river, then I can show you what a marvellous cook I am!'

It sounded very tempting—there were so few opportunities for much of a life outside the hospital. Lindy swept her eyes round the idyllic setting and sighed. Perhaps just a quick drink before she went back.

'Go on, then.' She smiled. 'If you're sure you can give up the time.'

She smiled up at him, her dark eyes sparkling and her cheeks slightly flushed from the walk she'd had. Her hair was shining blue-black, the slight wind lifting it in tendrils against her cheeks. Mike looked down at her for a second, an unreadable look in his eyes, then he gave a wicked chuckle.

'Might as well confess now. I didn't want to put you off coming, so I didn't actually bother phoning you about the cancelled meeting—thought I could tell you soon enough when you turned up!'

A flash of indignation flashed through Lindy as he disappeared into the cottage to get the drinks. He was doing it again! He'd deliberately engineered things, assuming that she had nothing better to do than turn up when there was no meeting at all! Talk about high-handed!

Mike looked at her sharply when he returned and handed her a glass of sparkling white wine. 'You look a bit fed up. What is it—would you like something else to drink?'

She took a sip of wine and looked at him coldly. 'Can't you guess? Don't you think I might just have liked the choice of an evening in? I've just finished night duty and, pleasant though this is, I could actually have done with an early night if there was one going! Next time, please, let me know if the meeting's cancelled—I don't really want anyone else organising my life!'

He firm mouth compressed, and an unreadable expression crossed his face, but he said in an even tone, 'Come on, let's not argue now. It's a lovely evening, and you don't have to stay long if you don't want to…we're probably both tired.'

He *did* look exhausted, thought Lindy guiltily, suddenly aware of the lines of weariness around his eyes, the slightly grey tinge to his face. Perhaps she was being selfish—the man had worked harder than anyone over the past ten nights, and she was thinking of her own precious feelings. Some women might have been flattered by his actions—but for her they'd just been a little too arbitrary.

She put a conciliatory hand on his arm. 'Sorry, you must be exhausted, too, Mike. It's just that I…well, I was expecting to discuss the ball with everyone.'

He nodded, shrugging slightly, and poured her another glass. He had become quieter, more remote than earlier.

'Why don't you show me the river walk before I go?' she said cheerily, trying to lift the atmosphere.

They finished their wine, and began to saunter through the field at the back of the cottage and down to the river, where a green beech wood came down to the path by the water. It was cool and shadowed under the trees and the ground sloped steeply down to the river. Mike walked slightly ahead of Lindy, and she wondered rather uneasily why he was distancing himself from her. Was he offended because of her reaction to the cancelled meeting? That was probably the reason, she reflected—sulking because she'd not leapt at the chance for them to be alone together!

It became very slippery and Mike turned and came back up the slope to offer her his hand over the most dangerous part. Suddenly she felt her feet slip away from her on a patch of damp mud, her flimsy sandals inadequately gripping the ground.

'Whoops!' she shrieked. She crashed against him, but he didn't flinch at the impact of her body on his. His hard frame braced easily against her. She was embarrassingly aware of the closeness of his bare muscled chest, the feel of the rough hairs of his arm on hers. Mike with no shirt on was even more attractive than fully clothed! He's going to think I slipped on purpose, Lindy thought with embarrassment as her heart beat a nervous tattoo against her ribs.

'Sorry!' she gasped. 'Lost my footing.'

How stupid of her to suggest this walk! She should have known that being alone with Mike was going to put her in a dangerous position from which she might not be able, or want to, extricate herself. All at once she was afraid—afraid of her ability to keep her distance from this man. The very thought of him making love to her sent a burning desire coursing through her, an irresistible longing to lie in his arms—she, who only a few weeks ago had vowed never to get close to men for a long, long time!

Mike kept his hand on her arm for a second, his eyes appraising her steadily. He didn't smile, but suddenly said, 'You know, there's so much I don't know about you yet. Perhaps now would be a good time to find out.'

Lindy smiled, trying to quell the butterflies still fluttering in her stomach and keep the mood light, less intense. 'You'd just discover how boring I was. I can't think of anything you'd find interesting about me.'

'That's where you're wrong,' he said harshly, putting his hands on her shoulders. 'Everything about you is fascinating to me—that's why I took the opportunity to see you alone tonight. I want to know all about you—what makes you tick...' He was silent for a moment then added rather deliberately, 'And why I seem to irritate you so much—like I obviously did this evening, for instance.'

She looked at him, taken aback by his sudden frankness, her hand nervously rubbing the old scar on her arm. There was some truth in what he'd said, only it was more annoyance than irritation!

'You don't...irritate me, Mike. It's just...just that sometimes you act...' She stopped, confused as to what she might say, trying to be tactful.

'How do I act?' he prompted, frowning at her.

She took a deep breath. 'Sometimes you act like Jake—the man that let me down.'

'It's that bad, is it?' He raised a quizzical eyebrow. 'I'm a rat like him?'

'No, of course you're not—you're not a rat. Oh, Mike, I only mean that sometimes I feel that I'm being taken over, not allowed to make my own decisions. I know I'm being hyper-sensitive—but if you'd been treated like I have then perhaps you'd be wary, too.'

Mike's eyes suddenly narrowed. 'For goodness' sake, play a different record, Lindy. You've got to learn to trust! I feel like I'm on trial the whole time— whatever I say may be taken down and used in evidence against me!' He gripped Lindy's shoulders and looked down at her, his eyes like blue chips of steel. 'You seem to want me to be something I'm not. I admit I do say things off the top of my head sometimes, but it doesn't mean I want to own you!'

Lindy flushed. 'I can't help it,' she said coldly. 'I'm not a machine. When I feel irritated I react, when a man makes decisions for me I feel resentful!'

Mike leant against the trunk of a tree by the path and watched her, a sardonic look on his face.

'I'm beginning to feel sorry for this Jake fellow,' he commented. 'You probably gave him too much aggro! Laying down rules to the person you love is death to romance, you know!'

A flood of anger washed over Lindy and she stared at him wordlessly for a minute. How *could* he say that—after what Jake had done to her?

'You know nothing about it!' she snapped. Unwarranted, a lump came to her throat and she turned away in confusion—where had all this come from? Somehow in the space of ten minutes the atmosphere had changed completely and now they seemed at daggers drawn!

She heard him sigh, then his arm pulled her round towards him, and the hard expression he'd had before had vanished. 'Then tell me, Lindy, tell me what he did to make you so suspicious of everything I say!'

His blue eyes were kindly as he looked down, and for a second she saw such affection in his expression that she forgot her quarrel with him. Perhaps she had been sharp when he'd been tired earlier—someone else might have taken what he did as a compliment! She flicked a rueful glance at him. Maybe it was time to tell him the full truth about Jake after all.

'You really want to know?' She sighed. 'Then I'll tell you.'

He pulled her down to sit beside him on a bank of dry leaves. 'You're sure you want to?' he said gently.

Lindy shrugged. 'Nothing to hide, really—just my shame that I was so crassly naïve.' She drew her knees up under her chin and stared into the distance.

'When you arrived,' she said haltingly, 'I was off men for ever! As you guessed, I had a boyfriend. In fact, just two weeks before you came I'd been engaged to Jake, a businessman, very successful and glamorous, as I've already told you.'

'And how did you meet this heartthrob?'

'I'd met him through work. He was a patient on a ward where a friend of mine nursed, and we started talking. He was very charming and persistent, but seemed lonely. He didn't know anyone round here, and was setting up an office in this area.'

'So you didn't know anything about his background—a little ominous!'

Lindy nodded. 'Easy to say with hindsight. He seemed to go away a lot with his work, conferences abroad—that sort of thing. I thought nothing of that, I was just so thrilled to have a high-profile man I loved and whom I thought would look after me.'

She paused and picked up a handful of leaves, watching them fall after she'd tossed them into the air, and Mike's arm crept round her comfortingly. 'Go on,' he whispered, 'I want to know everything.'

'At first it was fun to have a strong character who dominated me—I mistook domination for caring,' she added bitterly. 'We arranged the date of the wedding, the reception was booked. It was to be a quiet affair because I believed he was a widower, and I respected his wish to be low-key. Then by chance I called at his office one day unannounced. It was a shock to find his wife and two children had also come to see him! They had come over from Switzerland where he often went on business!'

Mike looked at her in astonished horror. 'What? My God, the low-life creep! He'd certainly pulled the wool over your eyes!'

Lindy shrugged. 'I was a fool. Perhaps I knew in my heart he was a shallow man who wanted power and someone to adore him unconditionally. He always had some odd excuse about us not making the engagement public "yet", so no one knew he was actually my fiancé. However, I really think he intended to go ahead and marry me bigamously—and if I hadn't found out we would have been married on the day you joined us on Casualty!'

'So,' he said slowly, 'on the day you were welcoming me, you should have been walking down the aisle… I can see why you were a mite stand-offish when we met! People like Jake give men a bad press!'

'He did behave rather badly,' Lindy said wryly.

Mike looked at her quizzically. 'And how do you feel about this man now?'

She was silent for a second, brushing a tendril of hair from her eyes. 'I don't know,' she said flatly. 'I think I feel numb about him. I know he told me lies, conned me, but it's hard to switch off completely so very soon. I suppose I feel bruised…'

'And convinced that all men are like him?' Mike smiled, a slightly wistful smile.

'It left me feeling wary, yes,' admitted Lindy. 'It was a lesson to me…'

Mike leaned forward and very gently took her face

between his hands and kissed her lips. 'Please, don't judge us all by Jake…' he whispered. His fingers traced a soft line from her jawline down her neck and the swell of her breasts. 'I want to make you forget that man,' he said huskily. 'I want to cure you of thinking that he's the norm….'

A warning shiver went through Lindy, but it was hard to resist when Mike's kisses became more insistent, and when she felt such incredible attraction for him. His fingers started to unbutton her blouse, and his arms pressed her gently back against the bank. She looked up at the canopy of green leaves arched above them, with the evening sun dappling through, and it was as if they were in their own intimate world, miles away from real life and anything to do with the hospital. Perhaps, she thought dizzily, the moment had come to try and forget about Jake…

Mike's body lay very close to hers, and his eyes were filled with a naked desire when they gazed down at her.

'Believe me, Lindy, *I* have no one else waiting in the wings,' he murmured. 'There's only you I want. You are so beautiful, your eyes are such a wonderful tawny colour.' He buried his face in her hair. 'And your hair smells sweet like new-mown hay…it feels just like silk. I want you so much—and I want you to feel the same. Allow me to make love to you, just a little…'

Her arms went round his neck in answer, and he lifted his powerful frame over her, straddling her body. She arched against him, feeling his need as much as her own, awed by her power to make him respond so ardently. His demanding lips started to kiss her frantically, her face, the hollow in her neck, the swell of her breasts. She felt them tingle as his hands explored her body, deftly undoing her pedal-pushers and slipping them down her legs.

Lindy felt her insides liquefy with desire as she lay before him clad only in the wispiest of bikini briefs. He knelt in front of her and silently gazed down at her slim but curvy, sun-dappled body. Then he bent down and kissed her stomach with the lightest of butterfly kisses until she moaned with longing.

'See how sweet this feels,' he murmured, his lips teasing hers apart and his tongue probing the secret recesses of her mouth. 'My beautiful Lindy, with this lovely sexy body.'

He gazed down at her, his blue eyes penetrating hers, making her feel she was drowning, her body responding and the soft contours of her flesh moulding themselves to his hard frame. His hands caressed every secret crevasse with gentle but insistent expertise. How easy it would be to capitulate completely, to give of herself as she had to Jake, so that in the end she became his possession, no longer her own woman... She tensed slightly at the thought, and moved her lips and face away from Mike's.

He opened his eyes and looked down at her, slightly puzzled, then with a ragged groan he rolled abruptly away from her, lying on his back and staring up at the trees.

'It's no good,' he muttered. 'I don't want to do anything while there's still someone else on your mind...'

Lindy blinked and looked at him lying beside her. This had happened before, Mike restraining himself almost at the height of passion.

'What do you mean....? What's wrong?' she whispered.

He turned his head and smiled wryly at her, his eyes

burning into hers. 'Nothing's wrong, nothing at all—far from it. But I had the feeling just then that—how should I put it? That I wasn't the only one on your mind!'

Lindy looked away. It was true, she thought miserably.

Mike propped himself up on one elbow and lay on his side, tracing the line of her jaw with one hand. 'Sweetheart, I don't want to force you to do anything. I want to make love to you more than anything in the world, but I shan't until I'm absolutely sure that all thoughts of Jake have been banished. I don't want to feel he's in the bedroom with us! At the moment I feel that man still occupies a corner of your mind. After all,' he continued gently, 'you compared me with him this evening…'

Lindy looked dazed, her heart still pounding from the arousal she felt. 'I try not to think of him,' she murmured.

His voice became rougher. 'I want you to admit that Jake is out of your life for ever and put the past behind you. You know in your heart you want to be with me, that we…belong together. It's been obvious to me for some time, but this phobia of yours for bringing Jake into the equation, well, it poisons what we could have together.'

She was silent. Mike was right. Wasn't there still a little part of her that thought of Jake, resented how he had treated her, and still feared another man could do the same? It would be so easy to capitulate, to admit that attraction was turning very fast to love with Mike, but, in all honesty, would it be fair to him at the moment?

A sudden light wind rustled through the branches of

the trees, and a low rumble of thunder sounded some miles away. Mike laughed, kneeling up and pulling her up against him. 'Don't worry, Lindy, I sense there's a change in the air…' He glanced up at the green panoply above them, then back at her, humour lurking in the blue depths of his eyes. 'And I don't just mean the weather!'

He folded her in his arms as the first big drops of rain began to fall. 'I'm not doing anything that you might regret later,' he said throatily. 'It would have been rather easy, I suspect, to have made love to you just now—but until I know that is what you really, really want, I'm holding back, my sweet. I want no ghosts between us—no secrets. I'm prepared to wait— but not for ever!'

Lindy gazed at him numbly, and swallowed. She *did* long for him—body and soul—but until the past had been exorcised from her mind, she could not truly give herself to Mike. She'd gone as far as telling him all about Jake, but there was still one secret in her life she could not tell him yet—and that was her meeting with Angela Lovatt!

The morning had seemed never-ending with a succession of varied cases, from a baby who'd swallowed a hairgrip to an elderly lady who'd fainted in a shopping mall. Lindy sipped her first coffee of the morning gratefully, glad of some time to herself. Her appointment in two days' time with Angela Lovatt was constantly whirling round in her head, and in some ways she wished she could talk to someone about this meeting. Mike's comments about having no secrets between them sprang to her mind, and she sighed. He would probably have advised her against delving into her childhood. Hadn't he said several times that she should put the past behind her?

Her heart thudded against her ribs at the memory of the other night. She still shuddered with longing when she thought of Mike's body moulded to hers, the passion of his kisses. He had been right about the reasons for her inhibitions, but somehow, by bringing them out into the open, she was beginning to see how illogical she was being. She knew she just had to stop comparing a man like Mike to Jake, or she would lose him for ever...

'Lindy, can you go up to Orthopaedics? The father of a patient—a Mr Romoli—wants to see you there.'

Lindy jumped out of her reverie as Janet put her head round the door.

'Do you remember the young Italian lad?' Janet said. 'Brought in here a few days ago after that group of cyclists were run into by the horse-box—he had multiple leg fractures.'

'Of course I remember him. He was worried what his parents would say about his crushed bike—they'd given it to him as a present!'

Janet nodded. 'Yes, that's the one. Mr Romoli is in the Italian diplomatic service and has to be back in London soon—wants to speak to you rather urgently.'

'What on earth for?' said Lindy, mystified. 'The boy...Carlo...he's OK, isn't he?'

'As far as I know. Take an early lunch-break and if you see that dozy porter, Jack, tell him I want him here pronto!'

To Lindy's surprise, Mike was part of the little circle round Carlo's bed, talking closely to a short, dapper man in a suit and the orthopaedic surgeon, Mark

Hadfield. Her heart thudded as she made her way to Mike's side, and his eyes locked with hers. For a second she was back in a green-leafed arbour of the woods. His powerful body was pressed to hers, his lips kissing her with fierce intimacy, and there was the pungent smell of rich earth all around them.

Mark Hadfield's brisk voice broke into her thoughts, and Lindy swallowed guiltily, a rosy blush covering her cheeks. Just as well no one could read her mind!

'Ah! Just the person!' he boomed. 'You remember Carlo, of course? I'm glad to say that we've patched up this young man beautifully, and he'll be ready to leave in a few weeks.'

Carlo, one leg held up in traction, grinned at Lindy and put two thumbs up in the air. 'Soon be on my bike again!'

Mark laughed, then shook an admonishing finger at the boy. 'Not too soon, my lad. Remember what I said—after those plasters are off, you do plenty of physio before you embark on any more races!'

He turned to Lindy, ushering her forward to the dapper little man. 'Sister, this is Mr Romoli, Carlo's father. He has a proposition to make to you and Dr Corrigan which I think you may find exciting!'

Lindy's eyes met Mike's, her mind whirling as to what the man should want with the two of them. Her mind flashed to various extraordinary possibilities, including suggesting that Mike and she set up a fracture clinic in Italy!

Mr Romoli gave a little bow and shook Lindy's hand. 'I am delighted to meet you, Sister Jenkins.' His accent was clipped, slightly sing-song. 'I have so much to thank you and Dr Corrigan for—you saved my boy's life.'

Lindy opened her mouth to protest that the surgeons had probably done more to help her son than they had, but he put up a forbidding hand. 'You are all so modest! I know better! And now I want to ask you a great, great favour.'

Lindy stared at him, baffled.

Mr Romoli's bright dark eyes twinkled at her. 'Don't be alarmed! My wife and I, we want to do something to show you how grateful we are, and this would help us as well. Carlo is going to be allowed home to Italy in four weeks. He insists he will be all right to travel alone on the plane—his mother and I don't think so. If you and Dr Corrigan would only accompany him to Rome, we should like you to have the use of our villa in the hills of Tuscany.'

Lindy gaped at the neat little man. 'But…why me?' she gasped, her heart racing with excitement, hardly able to believe that someone was offering a free holiday in Tuscany, a place she had always longed to visit.

'Mr Hadfield regrettably cannot go—he has family commitments. But our minds would be set at rest if we knew that you were going with our dear Carlo, and I believe that both you and Dr Corrigan have holiday due to you soon. It is a very large villa, so you would not bother each other, I'm sure. I have told him to take his sister and nephew—you also could ask anyone you pleased.'

Lindy's eyes caught Mike's for a second. His mouth quirked in a mischievous grin. 'I'm sure Sister Jenkins wouldn't bother us,' he said smoothly. 'In fact, it would add to the holiday if she was there…'

'Well?' twinkled Mr Romoli. 'What do you say?'

'It…it sounds absolutely fabulous,' Lindy stammered. 'I don't know what to say…'

'You will love it! It is set in olive groves and vine-yards on a hill, and there is a swimming pool—it can be very hot in June and July. From every aspect there is another hill with a beautiful ancient village on the top. So much to see and do!' He waved his hands expansively in the air, as if pointing out the delights he was mentioning.

Lindy felt dazed—it wasn't every day such a wonderful holiday was thrown into one's lap—but she and Mike together in such a romantic setting? She felt herself go hot at the thought—and would it be wise? Her mind flew back to the episode in the woods the day before, and Mike's remarks about Jake still influencing her.

'Perhaps,' she hedged delicately, 'I could think about it? It's so kind of you, and Tuscany is a place I've longed to go to all my life...'

'Well, then!' Mr Romoli beamed. 'No problem, eh?'

The scenario of lying by a sun-soaked pool, sipping Chianti and looking out over Tuscan hills made Lindy think very seriously that she might be mad to turn down the offer. But to be somewhere like that with Mike and maintain an aloof distance—impossible!

She flicked a glance at Mike as he chatted to Mr Hadfield, his tall figure bent slightly down to hear the surgeon, his dark hair just a little over his collar, and a picture of herself and Mike together under sun-kissed skies in Italy flashed enticingly before her, making her blood sizzle in her veins and her stomach turn over.

Mr Romoli clapped his hands briskly together, taking her silence for acceptance. 'So! I will arrange for the air tickets, for transport to our house in Rome to drop off Carlo, and then onwards to our place near the beautiful Iano—my secretary will contact you!'

The speed of the arrangements made Lindy feel rather dizzy, and Mr Romoli, looking at her doubtful face, reassuringly patting her hand. 'I think you are worried about sharing the holiday with Dr Corrigan if you hardly know him. I can assure you there is no need for you to meet at all in such a large place! You can have your friends—he can have his!'

Lindy swallowed. Mr Romoli was nearer to the truth than he realised! She *was* worried about sharing a holiday with Mike Corrigan—but not for the reasons the little Italian envisaged!

She blushed as Mike's mischievous eyes met hers. 'It will be a lovely opportunity for Sister Jenkins and I get to know each other a little better—not just as colleagues, Mr Romoli,' he said smoothly. 'I expect by the end of two weeks we'll all be very good friends indeed!'

CHAPTER EIGHT

LINDY took an exasperated look at the store cupboard she was busy checking—she couldn't wait to get away from ampoules of specialised drugs, sterile needles and sutures, but most of all patients! She could hardly believe that she had the prospect of spending a sunny holiday on the slopes of Tuscany in a few weeks. It seemed such a wonderful chance for Mike and herself to be together in a magical setting—even if his sister and nephew were there as well! Perhaps her fears about going away with him were groundless after all.

The bell rang from Reception, and Lindy tore her thoughts away from the magical idyll of drinking sparkling wine on a sun-soaked terrace. She sighed, plunging back to reality, and went to see what Jenny Forest, the receptionist, wanted.

An elderly man, supported on one side by Jenny and on the other by a young woman, was making his painful way down the corridor. He looked deeply anxious, but was querulously demanding that he be taken back home.

'Oh, come on, Dad,' encouraged the woman. 'I know you hate doctors, but you've got to see someone—you're in agony.'

'Never been in hospital in my life—and I'm not letting anyone fiddle about with me now!' he gasped.

He was beginning to struggle with the two women. Mike appeared from the small operations theatre. He went swiftly forward, quickly sizing up the situation, and took over from Jenny.

'Let me help you, sir,' he said gently. 'Why don't you just have a rest on the bed in this cubicle and allow us to have a very quick look at you?'

Lindy didn't think the old man would need much persuading, the sheen of perspiration on his forehead indicating the level of pain he was in.

'This is Mr Cunningham,' explained Jenny. She lowered her voice discreetly. 'His daughter's brought him in—she says he's suffering from retention.'

Mr Cunningham was helped up onto the bed, protesting weakly that 'it was all a fuss about nothing'. Mike put an arm on his shoulder and smiled understandingly at him.

'Let me guess, Mr Cunningham,' he said. 'I bet you didn't want to pass water all day yesterday, but perhaps you went for a pint last night and suddenly wanted to urinate, but nothing happened!'

Mr Cunningham looked at him in amazement. 'How did you know that?' he asked.

'It's quite a common thing in older patients, isn't it, Nurse? Sometimes your prostate gland swells up and blocks the entrance to the bladder—that's why you feel so uncomfortable. The nerves within the urinary tracts are less sensitive at your age, and that's probably why you didn't notice the build-up.'

'Well, I'm blessed,' remarked the old man, lying back on the pillows. 'I shouldn't have had that last pint, should I?'

He looked warily at Lindy as she took out a catheter from its wrapper. 'I don't like the look of that,' he muttered.

Lindy grinned reassuringly at him. 'When we've

cleared the passage to your bladder you'll feel like dancing a fandango,' she remarked. She turned to his daughter, who was looking almost as apprehensive as her father at the sight of the equipment Lindy was preparing.

'Why don't you go and have a cup of tea? This won't take long,' Lindy suggested tactfully.

His daughter looked relieved, and scuttled nervously out of the cubicle. Mr Cunningham made a valiant effort to sit up. 'I...I don't feel so bad now. I think I'll go,' he said querulously.

Mike sat by the bed and took the old gentleman's hand, and Lindy watched Mr Cunningham's anxiety subside slightly at his compassionate touch.

'In two minutes this will be over,' Mike promised, 'and you'll think you're in seventh heaven!'

A few minutes later Lindy went to Reception and tapped Mr Cunningham's daughter on the shoulder. 'Your father will be ready to go home soon,' she reported, 'and he says he feels as good as new!'

When the by now perky old man went out, he turned round and with a wink at Lindy said cheerily, 'You're right, love—I could do the eightsome reel at twice the speed now!'

'And that,' said Lindy to Mike, as they walked towards the canteen for lunch, 'is the good thing about A and E—making an old man like that very happy!'

He grinned. 'Certainly beats dealing with drunken oafs who've kicked each other senseless—I'd rather have a "bladder daddy" any day!' he observed.

He glanced out of the corridor windows at the sunny day outside. 'Let's go over to the park for a minute. I don't feel like sitting in that canteen longer than I need to—the smell of chips on a hot day is a bit of a turn-off. I'd rather talk about this proposed holiday in Tuscany somewhere else!'

As they crossed the road, he put an arm round Lindy's waist. 'Rather a switch of location, isn't it?' he murmured. 'From a woodland glade to dealing with prostate trouble in Casualty within two days—and I haven't stopped wanting to make love to you ever since!' He leaned forward and nibbled her ear gently, his lips forming a trail of fire down her neck.

'Are you crazy?' She giggled, gently disengaging herself. 'Supposing someone sees us? Do we want the whole of St Luke's knowing about us?'

'So what? I'll just make all the men envious! I thought we were getting on rather well the other night—just wanted to see if the magic was still working.' He grinned at her. 'I got the impression, young lady, that although I may have my faults, you weren't too averse to my company either!'

Lindy laughed outright, then looked at him impishly. 'What gave you that idea?'

'Well, the fact that you've agreed to come to Italy has reinforced it for one thing! And that reminds me,' Mike said softly, stopping for a second and pulling her round to face him, 'we've got some catching up to do between us—getting to know each other even better before we go, so that I'm the only one on your mind when we get there!'

She flushed slightly, her stomach somersaulting in a mixture of excitement and apprehension. 'I hope it works out all right,' she murmured. 'It sounds idyllic…'

'And so it will be,' he said firmly, bending his head to hers and kissing her hard on her lips. 'Whatever reservations you have, they'll have gone by then. By the way, I've organised something I think you'll like.'

What reservations could I have? thought Lindy weakly, that passionate kiss awakening fresh feelings of longing and desire. She smiled up at him. 'And what was this something you've organised?'

He looked rather pleased with himself. 'We both have a day off on Wednesday,' he said, 'and I thought I'd take you somewhere lovely in the country that I remember from my childhood. I'm having a picnic made up, and we'll get some air in our lungs, talk about the holiday.'

A shiver of disappointment went through Lindy. It sounded such a wonderful idea—alone with Mike for a whole day, with not a patient in sight—and she wouldn't be able to make it!

'I'm so sorry, Mike,' she said regretfully, 'I just can't do it then. I'd love to, really, but that day's impossible.'

He stared at her in astonishment. 'But it's our first free day! You can't have anything on then…'

'I'm afraid I've arranged something.'

Mike frowned, his eyes darkening. 'Well, un-arrange it, then. Look, we get so few opportunities when we're off together—I can't believe you can't make an effort and come.' He held her arms, squeezing them persuasively. 'Lindy, we need to spend time together—you know that. It's what we discussed the other night, when we were in the woods together.' His eyes burned down at her. 'I thought we'd reached a…loving agreement on that!'

'I just can't put it off,' she said stubbornly. 'It's impossible.'

A niggle of irritation went through her. A prior engagement was a prior engagement—and this one had taken all her courage to make. It was one of the most important meetings in her life, and no way would she cancel it.

She flashed him a slightly belligerent look. 'Mike, I'm not changing my mind. I can't let other people down.'

He shrugged his shoulders and stood back from her, looking at her with a faintly bitter smile.

'It sounds like the old, old story to me, Lindy. You're moving away from me again, aren't you? You're frightened to give completely of yourself, otherwise you'd realise that relationships are the most important things in life. I would give up anything for time with you...'

'It's not like that at all,' she said, her cheeks reddening. 'You know I want to be with you—after our lovely time the other night, the talk we had together, how could it be otherwise? But I can't just drop everything I planned. I have an important engagement—I'm not cancelling it.'

He looked at her curiously. 'Are you going for an interview—a new job or something?'

She shook her head. 'No, nothing like that.' She just couldn't tell him yet—she needed to keep this most personal of meetings private. Better to tell him after the event.

His mouth tightened, and he said tersely, 'Well, then, I know where I stand—rather low on your list of priorities!'

'Don't be so ridiculous!' Lindy looked at him angrily. 'Some things are so important they have precedence over everything. What about your first date with me—you stood me up because you had to help your sister, and that was quite understandable.'

'That was quite different. It was a last-minute emergency and I had no choice…'

'Neither do I,' said Lindy softly.

His eyes were blue chips of ice. 'We talked about not having secrets between us,' he commented coldly. 'If you don't want to confide in me—fine! But it's a fair indication that you want to keep me at arm's length, shut me out of your life!'

'Of course it doesn't mean that!' she snapped. 'You're just exaggerating wildly. Yes, there are some things in my life I want to keep to myself at the moment—why should I apologise for that? You're just too darned overbearing, Mike Corrigan!'

They glared at each other, Lindy reflecting bitterly that she'd been right after all. Mike Corrigan had a streak of arrogance within him. He was lovely, kind, wonderful—but thwart him at your peril when he wanted you to do something! Nevertheless, although she was simmering with indignation, she didn't really want to quarrel with him.

She sighed, and made an effort to be conciliatory. 'Maybe we could arrange it some other time, Mike.'
He nodded, but his voice was offhand, distant. 'Perhaps—I'll see you around!' Then he turned and walked back briskly to the hospital.

Lindy stared after him, a mixture of fury and frustration washing over her. She was *not* going to be owned by a man again! She wanted Mike like mad. She loved so much about him—his humour, talent and tenderness—but he had to learn that she had a life, too, otherwise the future between them looked bleak.

She pulled out her diary from her pocket and flicked

the pages to the appropriate date. 'Apsley Grange, Helmford,' she murmured to herself. 'I'll be there, Angela.'

Mike slumped in his chair in the office, gloomily looking at the view outside. Was he going completely mad? What in heaven's name had made him so incredibly selfish as to demand that Lindy give up her arrangements to go with him on their day off? How stupid and insensitive of him to assume automatically that Lindy would fall in with his plans! He cursed his impulsive nature. No wonder she was furious with him! Lindy was an independent girl who had her own life to lead. She'd made it clear that she needed her own space after this Jake man had broken her heart—and yet he couldn't resist trying to crowd her.

Mike gazed unseeingly at the medical article he was supposed to be reading, and felt a wave of shame go over him at the things he'd said to Lindy—that he was low down on her list of priorities, that she was bottling out of relationships! What possible right did he have to do that—just because he was falling head over heels for the girl and was crushingly disappointed that she couldn't spend the day with him?

'You fool, Mike Corrigan,' he murmured to himself. 'Trust you to go over the top!'

Things had started to go so well, he reflected sadly. He knew that she was attracted to him as much as he was to her, and he was sure that gradually her thoughts of Jake were starting to recede—she was learning that not all men were rats! And now, with the prospect of a wonderful holiday together in Italy, he had to go and blow it!

He sprang with frustrated energy out of the chair,

and punched one fist into his other hand with anger.
He'd take his nephew and sister out bowling on his day
off, he decided—anything rather than sit at home thinking of the mess he'd made between himself and Lindy.
But he wouldn't allow her to slip away from him. One
thing he knew for sure, the only way to make amends
would be to apologise—and fast! He vowed that the
first opportunity he got he would tell Lindy how sorry
he was about his behaviour.

Lindy's little car chugged up the long tree-lined drive
to the large house on the hill. Her hands gripped the
steering-wheel nervously, and her stomach somer-
saulted at the thought of the impending meeting. Was
she being a complete idiot in raking up the past? It
might all be a terrible mistake, and something she and
others would regret for evermore. But for so long she
had dreamed of this moment—she just *couldn't* give
up now!

There was the crunch of gravel as she parked before
the imposing building with its view over rolling parkland—what a magnificent place it was! She flicked a
look round, hardly able to believe that Angela Lovatt
lived in what could only be described as a stately home.
She pressed a large brass bell to the side of the huge
wooden door and pushed her hands in her pockets as
she waited, her heart thumping uncontrollably.

The click of footsteps could be heard coming towards the other side of the door, there was the sound
of a heavy lock being turned and the door swung
slowly open. A tall slim woman with dark hair and
wearing a beautifully cut cream trouser suit stood at
the entrance.

'I'm looking for Angela Lovatt.' Lindy's voice was almost a whisper.

The woman smiled rather tremulously. 'That's me.' There was a slight hesitation in her voice. 'Are you Madeline Jenkins?'

Lindy nodded.

The two women stared at each other for a second. For several seconds.

'Angela,' said Lindy at last, breaking the silence. 'I…I'm your daughter.'

The woman gazed at her with large dark eyes, then she stepped forward with her arms outstretched and enfolded Lindy in a passionate embrace, tears rolling down her cheeks.

'My darling child,' she whispered. 'If only you knew how I've longed to hear those words—at last my life is complete.'

It was like a dream, thought Lindy dazedly as she drove back to Manorfield from Apsley Grange that evening. She felt as if she'd been shaken by every kind of emotion. The missing part in the jigsaw of her life had been completed—and how glad she was that she'd had the courage to meet Angela.

Her thoughts turned to the woman who'd given her up for adoption over twenty years ago. She was everything she'd dreamed her natural mother would be— gracious, lovely and full of fun. It must have been as difficult for Angela as it had for her, she reflected, to be reunited with the child she'd last seen as a toddler. She recalled Angela's hesitant words to her when they'd gone into the magnificent drawing room and sat down together, Angela's eyes never leaving her daughter's face.

'What made you try to find me, Madeline?'

Lindy had started haltingly, then gathered confidence as she went on. 'When my adoptive mother was alive I never wanted her to feel that she wasn't everything I desired—I thought it might hurt her if I looked for you. She was a such a lovely person, but when she did die last year, the one thing that kept me going was that I might be able to trace you, and possibly find out more about myself.' She paused for a moment, then looked rather shyly at Angela. 'I was very worried about making enquiries. I knew it could be very awkward…for everyone involved—ghosts from the past, you know!'

Angela leaned forward and took Lindy's hand in hers. 'How glad I am that you did make the effort,' she said softly. 'I never kept any secrets from Bernard—my husband.' She gave a sudden little laugh. 'I suppose he's your stepfather now! I told him when he married me that I'd had a baby girl when I'd been seventeen, and she'd been adopted…' She paused for a second, twisting the beautiful rings on her hand nervously. 'I longed more than anything else to try and find you, but we knew that unless you contacted us first it would be the wrong thing to do. You had to want to find me.'

They smiled at each other, each hardly able to believe that they'd finally met. Then Lindy swallowed, longing to ask a difficult question.

'Can I ask…why couldn't you keep me?'

Angela pressed her hands together as if suppressing great emotion. 'It…it wasn't easy, Lindy, darling—it was the hardest thing I ever did in my life. You see, your father was my parents' greatest friend, and it was totally taboo that he should have abused their trust and had an affair with me. Shortly after I discovered I was pregnant he was killed in a car crash, and I didn't know how to deal with the situation. My parents were very strict, and I just couldn't tell them about it. I decided the only thing to do was to take up my place at art school and have the baby secretly when I was there.'

'You must have been so lonely,' whispered Lindy, her eyes filling with tears. 'How did you cope?'

Angela nodded. 'I did feel very lonely—there were agencies around that helped unmarried mothers, but not as many as there are today. I was determined that when you were born I was going to bring you up myself—unfortunately, things don't always work out as one hopes.'

'What happened?' Lindy leaned forward, fascinated by the story.

'I was desperately ill after I had you, and spent a long time in hospital. Of course my parents discovered what had happened. They were adamant that you should be adopted, and although I was in no fit state to fight I was desperate to keep you. I'm afraid I fell out with them and never saw them much again after that. But your welfare was my prime interest and I decided that, for your sake, the only thing to do would be for you to be fostered until I was in a position to look after you.'

Angela sighed. 'I couldn't bear to give you up for adoption immediately. I was hoping and praying I'd eventually be able to look after you. That's why you went for the first few years to Oaklands Home—I used to visit you there.'

'I remember Oaklands Home,' said Lindy with a smile. 'I remember having an accident there and hurting my arm.' She pulled up her sleeve and showed Angela the scar.

Angela stroked it softly. 'You poor little thing... Such a lot happened to you that I never knew...' She gathered herself together and continued with her story. 'I began to realise that I was depriving you of the family life I'd hoped I could give you—I never seemed to be able to get myself on an even keel—and that's when you went to the mum and dad you grew up with, although it nearly killed me when you went away.'

She studied Lindy's face lovingly. 'And I think they did a wonderful job with you,' she said softly. 'My beautiful baby has grown up into a beautiful woman with a wonderful career—I couldn't be prouder of you, darling.'

A sudden rush of affection flowed through Lindy for this woman she'd never known, but had thought about all her life. Angela had sacrificed so much so that she, Lindy, would have a decent life. She leaned forward and kissed Angela's cheek.

'I'm lucky I had two good mothers,' she murmured.

A cough from the doorway made them both turn round. A tall, distinguished-looking man stood there, looking slightly anxious.

'All right to come in?' he asked in a rather gruff voice.

Angela jumped up and went over to him, pulling Lindy along with her. 'Bernard, darling, this is Madeline—the daughter I've been longing to introduce you to ever since you and I married!'

Bernard Lovatt's face was wreathed in smiles as he held Lindy's hand, his expression full of kindness and affection. 'This is a wonderful day for us,' he said simply.

Angela gave him a loving look. 'Bernard and I have been married fifteen years—he was my boss at the architects' firm I worked for. I used to worship him from afar, never dreaming that such a handsome bachelor would notice me!'

He laughed. 'That was just a ploy to catch you— playing hard to get!' He added seriously, 'It was the best day of my life when I married Angela—and I don't think we've had a cross word!'

Lindy looked at the handsome couple with admiration, not untinged with envy. This was how marriage should be—total trust between two people, a loving relationship in perfect balance. Would she—could she—ever dare to think that things between her and Mike might work out like that?

'Do you have children yourselves?' she asked, putting Mike out of her mind for the moment.

Angela and Bernard looked at each other with a slightly sad smile, then Angela sighed. 'Unfortunately, I wasn't able to have any more babies after you. We hoped—but none came along.'

'Until you turned up,' said Bernard gently. 'I think the daughter we've been longing for has finally arrived!'

The afternoon passed in a blur of excited talk— catching up on twenty missing years took a long time. At length, Lindy said she'd have to go, although Angela and Bernard begged her to stay.

'I have to get back,' said Lindy regretfully. 'I'm on duty in the morning.'

'You'll come back next Friday, won't you, darling? We still have so much to tell each other. And, of course, it's a very special day—your birthday!' Angela looked pleadingly at Lindy. 'For many, many years it's been such a sad day for me. This year it could be one of the happiest in my life, spending some of that day with you! Do say you'll come after work—after all, we're only twenty miles away from Manorfield!'

Lindy hugged them both, and promised to come back for dinner the next week. She left, feeling a singing happiness inside her that she'd met two very special people—and now they were part of her life!

Gradually, as she drove away, the happy euphoria bubbling inside her began to fade slightly. The silly quarrel she'd had with Mike about not being able to go on a picnic with him still rankled at the back of her mind. She had been right, she thought defiantly, to keep that part of her life to herself. Meeting her mother could have been a disaster and something she would have wanted to forget about.

Now, if Mike and she hadn't quarrelled she would have been dying to tell him about finding her lovely mother after all these years and discovering her background. But now, despite her overwhelming attraction for the man, wasn't that clash between them a warning that she might slip back into the same situation she'd been in before—constantly deferring to a man who wanted his own way?

Moodily she changed gears as she turned into her road. In a few weeks she was supposed to be going to Italy—would she and Mike be talking by then? Perhaps making up with Mike might not be the wisest thing she could do!

Mike slung himself down on the sofa and took a gulp of whisky. He'd got through the day all right—his nephew had enjoyed the bowling, and his sister had relished the chance of sharing the responsibilities of a young child with her brother. But it hadn't been easy to maintain a carefree manner when all the time he'd been cursing himself for his stupidity with Lindy. While he'd been hurling balls down the bowling lane, or eating copious amounts of fish and chips, at the back of his mind he'd been reliving that awful scene with her.

He swirled the golden liquid gloomily in the glass— he had to repair things between them at the earliest opportunity: He loved her, dammit, and just as it seemed he'd begun to cure her of her wariness of men, he'd demonstrated just how boorish he could be!

He thought about when he could make his apologies—tomorrow would be difficult because the St Luke's appeal was to be televised on a local news programme, and he was being interviewed. That would probably take up most of the morning, and there was some sort of training programme in the afternoon that Lindy might be attending. Nevertheless, he thought grimly, swallowing the last of the whisky in one gulp, as soon as he could be alone with Lindy he was going to mend fences.

CHAPTER NINE

THE huge Victorian hall of St Luke's seemed to have been transformed into a large stage. A television camera was trained in front of the impressive sweeping staircase where Tessa Martin, the local television presenter, was preparing to interview staff in connection with the hospital appeal. There were wires snaking across the floor and microphones dangling above people's heads. Some of the hospital staff were grouped in a corner, watching the proceedings on a large screen monitor at the side, and Lindy recognised various staff who were being briefed by a girl with a clipboard.

Lindy watched with amusement as Jack Hulse vigorously combed his hair before going on camera and giving his version of what a hospital porter's job was. And, of course, as prime mover in the effort to raise money, there was Mike Corrigan, obviously just in from Casualty with his hospital greens still on and a stethoscope dangling round his neck.

'Wow!' murmured a young nurse as Mike was brought forward in front of the cameras. 'I'm going to transfer to A and E as soon as possible! I obviously chose the wrong department!'

There was a little snicker from her companions, and the girl with the clipboard shot a warning look towards them, putting a finger on her lips.

Mike was talking to the presenter and Lindy swallowed hard. The darned man looked too much like a television soap doctor to be true! He seemed twice as tall beside the tiny figure of Tessa Martin, his wide smile and brilliant eyes translating so photogenically to the monitor screens—it wasn't fair that one man should have so much! She closed her eyes for a moment and swayed slightly. Could it really be true that a short while ago he had been in the woods with her, his body on top of hers, kissing her frantically and arousing her as no other man had ever done?

She felt herself blushing at the memory, and opened her eyes, crushingly aware of the present situation between them. It was going to be pretty difficult to work with Mike at the moment after their frosty parting the other day. Then she lifted her chin defiantly. The quarrel had not been of her making—he had been to blame!

'Excuse me—can I have a quick word?'

Lindy blinked. The girl with the clipboard was standing in front of her, a winning smile on her face.

'Hi! I'm Sandy Lockwood, the floor manager. Dr Corrigan tells us that you work in A and E with him and that you've been on the fund-raising committee. He thinks you should be in on the interview, too!'

Lindy flashed a cold look at Mike. 'Surely it doesn't need both of us,' she protested. 'I'd just be repeating what he said.' Typical, she thought, crossly. He tells them I should be interviewed without asking me first!

'But it's so much more interesting if we get some dialogue on your work generally, and why you think the hospital should stay open.' insisted the girl. 'Go on, you're a natural for the screen with those big eyes and lovely dark hair—the two of you would look superb together. Just what we need—the doctor-and-nurse team thing!'

Lindy's face turned crimson with embarrassment, suddenly aware that Mike's gaze was boring into her back as he listened to Sandy's enthusiastic persuasion. She opened her mouth to protest, but before she could object, Tessa Martin's arm was round her waist, drawing her in front of the cameras and beside Mike.

'Here we have two heroes of the A and E Department,' she gushed. 'Dr Mike Corrigan and Sister Lindy Jenkins—at the very cutting edge of medicine, dealing with the shattered bodies of Manorfield that come into the hospital day in and day out!'

Lindy felt a gurgle of hysterical laughter starting to erupt from her stomach at this dramatic introduction and the situation she'd found herself catapulted into!

'I suppose you all work very much together—as a team?' Tessa was saying.

'Oh, yes…very much as a team,' Lindy murmured, shooting a quick glance at Mike.

Tessa turned to Mike. 'I believe you worked in New York before you came to Manorfield. How does working at St Luke's compare to the Big Apple?'

'St Luke's is smaller, but it's just as vital to the community, providing a wonderful local service—I'm glad to say we've managed to raise almost three quarters of the money needed to keep it open. Hopefully local businesses will help with the rest.'

'I expect they welcomed someone with your experience with open arms!'

Tessa smiled brilliantly at Mike, and his eyes flicked over the bright lights and looked directly at Lindy for a few seconds. 'People have made me very welcome— I've made the odd gaffe here and there, but hopefully I can sort things out!'

Lindy felt her heart skip a beat—was that a coded message of apology? Tessa Martin laughed roguishly at them both. 'And in your busy lives is there any time for, shall we say, socialising? To the general public of course, doctors and nurses seem to lead rather glamorous and intense lives—is that so?'

A crimson flush spread over Lindy's cheeks, and Mike grinned wickedly at the presenter. 'I can't say there aren't temptations but, of course, our patients come before romance—in the hospital anyway. Isn't that right, Sister?' His eyes locked with Lindy's for an instant. She bit her lip, half inclined to laugh, half astounded at his nerve!

The interview was over, and Lindy blew out her cheeks with relief—standing next to Mike in that chummy situation had been a little difficult to say the least. She needed a cup of strong coffee before starting back to work.

'Lindy,' said a deep, urgent voice, 'I want a word with you. We need to talk.'

Lindy's heart clanged against her ribs and she whipped round quickly to face Mike. From his face she could see it wasn't going to be a professional discussion.

'Please,' she said quickly, 'not just now, not with all these people around…'

Mike looked impatiently at the crowd of people jostling around them, making their way back to the wards, and he cursed softly. 'For heaven's sake—it's impossible to be in this place without a cast of thousands filling every corner. Meet me in the office in a few minutes—I must speak to you.' His eyes blazed down at her, a kind of desperation in their depths. 'Please, be there, Lindy. I've got to explain something…'

His hands were on her shoulders, their touch making her nerve endings tingle. He started to pull her closer, as if he was going to embrace her right there, in front of everyone! She pulled away firmly, but nodded agreement at his suggestion.

'Just for a minute, then,' she murmured, wondering just what he had in mind to say to her.

Mike was waiting for Lindy in the office, leaning back against the desk. He got up and closed the door as she came in.

'This won't take long, will it, Mike?' she asked. 'Someone could come barging in...'

'Don't worry.' He grinned slightly. 'I've put a notice on the door—SHORT TRAINING SESSION IN PROGRESS. That should give us a little time!'

His expression changed. 'Lindy,' he said, his voice slightly rough. 'We need to talk things through. We parted on a bad note the other day—you were rather cross with me.'

Lindy shrugged. 'I had reason to be, don't you think? It was you that flared up, insisting I give up my arrangements—right? I do have a life of my own, you know!'

He nodded ruefully. 'OK—I was totally out of order. I didn't mean to harry you—to act like the infamous Jake! All I wanted was some time for us to be alone together for once...not just a snatched hour or two in the evening. Can you understand that?'

His arms were on her shoulders and they were standing so close, hip to hip, his face a few inches from hers. It was hard for Lindy to resist winding her arms round his neck and pressing her body to his, but for once she held back. Was this going to be a regular occurrence—Mike apologising for his high-handed behaviour, her forgiving him?

She stepped back and looked at him coolly. 'You're used to getting your own way, aren't you, Mike?'

His eyes swept over her tall, beautifully poised figure, those wonderful tawny eyes looking at him defiantly, and he smiled faintly. 'You know I'm slightly impulsive, prone to speaking my mind.'

Lindy shrugged her shoulders. 'I'm afraid it doesn't work with me, Mike… I don't like to be pushed around. I even found myself giving a television interview this morning because of you!'

He dismissed that with a shrug. 'That was nothing to do with our personal life,' he countered. 'That was in our professional capacity!'

'I still like to make my own choices,' retorted Lindy.

Mike held his hands up in supplication. 'I know, I know,' he said contritely. 'It's just that, well, the other day I saw an opportunity for us to be spend quality time together—seemed a waste of a day off not to use it. I admit I was a bit heavy-handed but, for heaven's sake, we'd just agreed that we should spend more time together before we go to Italy…'

'Perhaps that isn't such a good idea after all,' snapped Lindy. 'I want to relax on holiday, not feel I've got to do what others want me to all the time.'

'It wouldn't be like that,' Mike said fiercely. His hands held hers firmly and he pulled her towards him. 'You could be as independent as you wanted,' he rasped, his cobalt blue eyes holding hers unflinchingly so that her stomach did a sudden somersault. 'Just think, Lindy, having a drink of perfectly chilled white wine under a blue sky, high on a hill overlooking the valley—and not a patient in sight!'

She smiled faintly, and a sweet longing swept through her to be friends with him again and allow him to hold her once more. It would be so easy to forgive and forget and tell him about her new-found mother

and why she hadn't been able to go with him the previous day. Then she thought crossly. Why should she
let him off the hook so easily? She was sick of being
dictated to!

The shrill noise of the telephone cut harshly into her
thoughts, and she grabbed it almost gratefully—she
wouldn't have to make any decisions just now!

It was Janet on the phone. 'Ah, there you are!' her
gruff voice barked down the line. 'Could you find Mike
and ask him to examine a fifteen-year-old girl complaining of abdominal pain? She needs to be looked at
now. Her name's Mary Percival—cubicle four.'

'Looks like our "training session" has to end,' said
Lindy, a feeling of relief sweeping over her that her
meeting with Mike was over before it got too intense.
'Janet wants you to see a teenage abdominal patient.'

'Damn it,' muttered Mike as he followed her out.
'Am I never going to get the chance to talk to you
alone?' He bit his lip and sighed. It was evident that
Lindy wasn't going to be won back too easily.

The young girl in cubicle four looked terrified, but her
mother was doing her best to remain calm in front of
her young daughter. She was the kind of down-to-earth,
sensible woman one would imagine to be a perfect
mother reflected Lindy, probably running the Guides or
the PTA and the first to volunteer to make cakes for a
fund-raising coffee morning.

'I had to collect Mary from a netball match at
school,' the mother said with a worried frown. 'The
teacher thought she might have appendicitis, but she
had her appendix out years ago.'

Mike took a shrewd look at the young girl, at her
extreme pallor and the beads of sweat on her forehead.

'She seems in acute shock,' he murmured to Lindy, before turning kindly to Mrs Percival. 'I just want to take a few notes from Mary and examine her. Perhaps you'd like to wait in Reception, have a cup of tea from the machine there and try and relax for a minute?'

The teenager groaned and clutched her mother's hand. 'Don't go, Mum,' she pleaded. 'Stay here with me—it's such agony.'

Mike caught Lindy's eye. Sometimes it was better that Mum left—a young patient was often inhibited about giving full histories if parents stayed!

Lindy put a comforting hand on Mary's arm. 'Don't worry, Mary,' she soothed. 'We'll find out what's wrong—it's amazing what we can find out from scans and other tests—but it's really best if your mum has a break for a few minutes. It won't take long, and then we can do something for the pain.'

Her voice had the firm ring of pleasant but quiet authority, and Mrs Percival nodded obediently. After dropping a swift kiss on her daughter's cheek, she left the cubicle.

'Thanks, Sister,' murmured Mike, his glance catching Lindy's for an instant. He turned kindly to the frightened teenager. 'I'm just going to feel your tummy, Mary—I'll be very gentle. Just try and straighten up for a minute.'

Mary tensed visibly. 'Something's wrong,' she whispered. 'I know it—it's killing, this pain.'

'I know, I know, Mary—hang on in there for a second,' murmured Mike, palpating the tense lower and upper abdomen for a few seconds. Then he straightened up and pulled a blanket back over the girl.

'As Sister told you, we might do a scan which could show an ovarian cyst. But there are other conditions which might cause this pain. I notice you're having a period,' he observed. 'When was your last one?' His voice was so gentle and matter-of-fact that the young girl wasn't a bit embarrassed.

Mary frowned. 'About two or three weeks ago. But it's nothing like a period pain, it's much much worse than that!' She groaned again, and drew up her knees to her chest.

'I don't think it's a period pain.' Mike's eyes flicked across to Lindy, and she gave a little nod. He obviously had a suspicion as to the cause.

'Mary,' he said gently, 'is there the slightest chance you could be pregnant?'

The girl looked wide-eyed at Mike and Lindy. 'What do you mean?' she whispered. 'Of course not! I'm having a period, aren't I? So I can't be pregnant.'

Mike gave a barely perceptible nod to Lindy, and she sat down in the chair beside Mary and took her hand. 'It might not be a period, love,' she explained. 'It could just be that you're bleeding from one of your Fallopian tubes—they are the tubes that lead from your uterus.'

'Why should it bleed?'

'Occasionally a fertilised egg can lodge there. As it gets bigger, it ruptures the surrounding tissue—that's why we've got to find out if you're actually pregnant. We can do that by giving you a pregnancy test and an ultrasound scan.'

Mike cut in gently, 'We're concerned that you might have what we call an ectopic pregnancy. Could that be possible, Mary?'

Mary sat upright, wincing in pain as she did so. Her voice was hardly a whisper. 'No...yes.' She drew a deep breath. 'Perhaps… But I didn't know I could get pregnant…so easily. We only sort of did it the once…'

Her voice trailed off, then she put her hands over her face and burst into tears. Lindy passed the girl a paper handkerchief and Mike stood quietly by.

'Mary,' she said softly, 'I know it's difficult, but we'll have to tell your mother…'

'No!' cried Mary hysterically. 'She'll go ballistic! Don't let her know…' The teenager started sobbing desperately and Lindy put her arm round her.

'Look, whatever's happened, I guess your mum will stand up to the shock,' she said reassuringly. 'She wants you to be well—this is a problem that can't be ignored.'

'She…trusted me, told me all about sex and things… I've let her down.' She turned her face from Lindy to the wall and sobbed silently.

'I'll go and arrange for a bed in Obs and Gynae, and for the consultant to do a scan and possibly a laparoscopy,' said Mike in a low voice. He glanced at Mary's hunched little figure.'You're doing a grand job, Lindy—keep talking to her!'

It was funny how praise from Mike made her heart sing, thought Lindy wryly as he went out. Whatever her feelings about him romantically, she had nothing but the highest respect for him professionally. She turned her attention back to Mary.

'Look, Mary, we don't know for sure it's an ectopic pregnancy, but if it is, although it's very sad, it means you can start again. You'll have learnt something from it, won't you? You'll know that unprotected sex can lead to pregnancy and, of course, disease.'

Gently she turned the girl's anguished face towards her. 'Your mum has to know what's the matter with you some time, lovie. Would you like me to mention it to her first? She's not the first person I've had to tell this sort of news to.'

'Would you? Would you really? I don't think I could find the words…'

It was as Lindy had thought—Mrs Percival, after the initial shock and disbelief that her little girl could possibly be pregnant, was mainly concerned with her child's health.

She heaved a sigh, and gave Lindy a wry smile. 'You think you've told them everything, warned them of all the dangers, and still they get themselves into all kinds of trouble!' she said sadly.

After Mary Percival had been taken up to the ward, Lindy walked slowly back to the office, her thoughts automatically turning back to Mike and his attempts to justify his actions the other day. Her mind whirled in a confusion of emotions. She supposed that he'd been trying to apologise for his behaviour, whilst still maintaining that he had cogent reasons for behaving so boorishly! And yet…and yet she felt so much for him, could barely think of him without yearning for his touch, the feel of his passionate body on hers. Perhaps it was stupid of her to compare him with Jake, when she knew how kind and gentle he could be, so thoughtful.

'Lindy, there's a patient in the waiting room wants to see you. Can you go and shut him up? He's been triaged, but is making a fuss about having to wait. Says you're a friend, and obviously thinks you can get him to the top of the queue!'

The harassed figure of Jenny Forest, the receptionist, stood in front of her. She had to bear the brunt of a lot of aggravation in the first instance, as persistent patients seemed to think it was her fault they weren't being seen immediately. She lived on her nerves and copious quantities of black coffee.

'What's his name?' asked Lindy, wondering which friends of hers would dare use her to try to get ahead in the queue!

'Burton—Jake Burton. He's hurt his ankle.'

Lindy stopped dead, and her face flushed a deep crimson. She could hardly believe what she was hearing. '*What?*' she spluttered. 'Did you say Jake Burton?'

Jenny looked at her in surprise. 'Yes, you do know him?'

Lindy gritted her teeth. 'Yes, I do know him,' she said grimly. 'And I can't wait to sort him out!'

She marched briskly towards the reception area, her blood boiling, unable to believe that the man she might have married only a few weeks ago should actually have had the cheek to use her name to gain himself some advantage in his treatment! What was more incredible, she had only just been comparing Mike to him!

She stood at the entrance to the reception area and looked over to where he was sitting, in the front row. He looked just the same, well dressed in an expensive designer suit, fairish hair cut slightly too long—and a petulant expression on his face. He was saying something angrily to Jenny and pointing to his watch with vicious stabbing motions. Lindy took a deep breath and walked over to him.

'Hello, Jake. I believe you wanted to see me?' she said coolly.

He looked up at her, and the old charming smile lit up his face.

'Ah, Lindy!' he murmured. He held out his hand

towards her. 'How wonderful you look! I knew you'd come and rescue me!' His eyes swept in an intimate way over her trim figure. 'You know, sweetie, I still miss you so much—'

'What's happened to you?' butted in Lindy tersely.

His look turned to patient suffering. 'I'm in unbelievable agony here. I was playing golf yesterday and twisted my ankle, getting out of a bunker. Today it's ballooned up and I can hardly walk on it—probably broken something.' An aggrieved look crossed his face. 'Can you get me seen now, please? These dolts seem to think I've all day to waste!'

Lindy tried to control her temper with difficulty, her cheeks colouring with the effort, and Jake replaced the charming smile on his face. 'I hope you've managed without me, Lindy—are you still cut up about it all?'

Lindy was glad to be able to speak with perfect candour. 'No, Jake, I'm intensely relieved. It would have been the biggest mistake in my life to have married you.' She looked down scornfully at him. 'I imagine the triage nurse has assessed your injury?'

Jake frowned. 'If you mean that bad-tempered kid who told me there were other, more urgent cases than mine, yes, she did! That's why I called for you—can you deal with it now? You know what a busy fellow I am. I've got clients coming to see me in half an hour.'

'I'll just go and see the triage nurse for one second.'

Sheila was on triage duty. She looked angrily at Jake when Lindy questioned her about him.

'Yes, he's got a bad sprain. He's going to need an X-ray just in case he's cracked anything but, of course, he's way down the list—we've got a coronary patient and a bad RTA on their way. I've never met such a rude, pushy man!'

Lindy grinned at her. 'Well said! I'll go and spell it out to him.'

'So? Have you sorted it out, then, my love?' Jake's handsome but slightly fleshy face looked up at Lindy, confident in the knowledge that he would be getting what he wanted.

'Yes, of course, Jake.' She smiled down at him sweetly. 'The estimated time you'll be seen is three hours. People are seen in strict order of the seriousness of their condition—I can't change that.'

His face went red, and he made a half move to get up. 'What? This is preposterous—what kind of outfit is this anyway?' His charming expression had been replaced by a belligerent scowl.

'I'm sorry, Jake, I'm needed urgently back there—there's some very ill patients to be looked after.' She cocked her head to one side, looking at him provocatively. 'You know, Jake, you've put on a bit of weight since I saw you last—just free advice! Stay off the fatty foods and drink less—you'll feel better for it!'

She turned on her heel and walked lightly away, a tremendous urge to laugh welling up inside her and a sense of satisfaction that a bully had been bested!

She flicked a quick look behind her before she turned the corner—he had heaved himself up and was limping towards the exit. A sudden and wonderful observation came to her—it was as if a window had been cleaned after a storm, and she was able to see through it clearly for the first time. Mike Corrigan was *nothing* like Jake Burton! How could she *ever* have thought there was any resemblance to that rat she'd once been engaged to? She almost gasped with relief. She must have been completely mad to think that Mike—darling, sweet

Mike—had any of Jake's bombastic ways! The two men were as different as chalk and cheese, and it had taken this chance meeting with Jake to open her eyes to that!

CHAPTER TEN

IT HAD been a hectic week, filled for Lindy with frustration and longing to see Mike. The irony was that the moment she realised just how much she cared for him he should be attending an accident and emergency conference in the North of England for a few days! She couldn't wait to let him know in no uncertain terms that Jake was out of her life and mind for good.

Since her unexpected meeting with Jake the scales had finally dropped from her eyes, and she'd seen the man for what he was. How could she have ever thought that Mike bore any resemblance in character to Jake? Jake's spurious good looks and powerful business image were just a façade to hide a selfish character, solely concerned with his own needs. She must have been completely blind to ever have been attracted to such a man!

She realised that her unhappy experiences had probably contributed to her paranoia about getting entangled in an unsatisfactory relationship again—and Mike had recognised that. She blushed when she thought of how understanding Mike had been—and how patient! Perhaps, she reflected wistfully, he would ring her that weekend and they could spend quality time together. Surely he wouldn't give up on her, even if she had been short with him the other day!

But now, thank heavens, it was the end of Friday afternoon, and she was going to see Angela and Bernard that evening to celebrate her birthday. She couldn't wait to see them again and hear more about her family background. She'd brought a change of clothes and would go straight from the hospital after a shower. She marched briskly into the staffroom to pick up her things from her locker.

'Surprise, surprise! Happy birthday, Lindy!'

An explosion of giggles and laughter erupted from the small room and Lindy gave a start of surprise as a sea of faces looked back at her.

She gazed round in astonishment, then laughed as the assembled little crowd burst into a ragged rendering of, 'Happy Birthday to You'.

'What the...? Oh, you idiots—can't a girl keep a secret any more?'

Sheila was the only person who knew when her birthday was and Lindy shot her a mock-baleful look and growled at her, 'I'll see you later, you wretch!'

Sheila held out a cake with a large lit candle in the middle of it, and brandished a huge card signed by everyone in the department.

'Don't blame me for the surprise party.' She grinned. 'It was Mike who made the arrangements when I told him it was going to be your birthday!'

Lindy's heart did a perfect swallow dive into her stomach then soared up again—Mike must have come back early from the conference and was here after all! She flicked a glance round the room and, sure enough, there he was at the back of the crowd, his tall figure visible above everyone else, looking absolutely heart-stoppingly handsome. She could hardly stop herself from forcing her way through to him and flinging her arms round his neck! Never had she wanted a roomful of people to disappear so much!

'Come on, Lindy, let's have some of this wine,' said

Sheila. 'After the day I've had, I could drink the whole bottle!'

'Oh, yes, please!' Carrie appeared eagerly at Lindy's side. 'Surely we deserve it now!'

Lindy sighed. Cosy tête-à-têtes with Mike would have to wait…the next half-hour was taken up with happy chatter. Lindy was constantly aware that Mike was in the room—and yet he hadn't come up to her like everyone else had. She flicked a cautious look at him—he was probably not sure of the reception he'd get. After all, when he'd tried to apologise, she'd been less than gracious. She gritted her teeth in frustration— she had to find a quiet moment to tell him now that things were different and that she wanted their romance to go full steam ahead!

Then all at once he appeared at her side, looking down at her with his heavenly deep blue eyes. 'Happy birthday,' he murmured. 'I hope you don't mind about this?' He swept his hand around the room at the little crowd. 'Seemed too good an opportunity to miss—especially as I know you probably don't want to come out to dinner with me alone tonight!'

Lindy flushed. Oh, how she longed to be alone with him! Perhaps not tonight—she would be with Angela and Bernard—but any other time in the whole year!

'That would have been lovely, Mike,' she started.

'But you can't!' he finished flatly. 'Don't worry, Lindy, I understand.' He bent down to her and kissed her softly full on the lips. 'Just claiming my birthday kiss,' he murmured.

They gazed at each other, both shocked by the sudden physical contact, his eyes burning into hers with passionate intensity. Lindy struggled to keep calm in the midst of the babble surrounding her, although she felt familiar little shocks running through her body in response to his touch. He stood directly in front of her, blocking out the rest of the room. The background buzz of conversation faded, and it seemed to her there were only two people there at the moment—Mike and herself!

He put his hand in his pocket and pulled out a little package. 'I thought this might be a reminder of some happy times we've had.'

He placed it in her hand then, putting both hands behind her neck, drew her face towards his and kissed her harder this time, almost savagely. 'Happy birthday,' he whispered.

Lindy gasped at the brutal intensity of his kiss, and she touched her lips, throbbing with that assault on them. She was suddenly uncomfortably aware of the other people around them and drew back slightly. Then she looked down at the little box and opened it. Nestling in the box was the little figure of an athlete on a golden chain.

'Oh!' she gasped in delight. 'You didn't need to do this—but it's lovely!'

'Memories of the fun run.' He smiled. 'And especially what came afterwards. A little farewell gift.'

She looked at him baffled. A 'farewell gift'? The words resonated in a horrible way round her head—had she heard aright?

'W-what?' Her voice trembled, unable to believe what she'd heard. 'What are you talking about?'

He smiled rather sadly. 'I don't blame you for not falling over backwards to accept my apologies the other day,' he said. 'I've been thinking about how I must seem to you—overbearing and demanding. After what you've been through, that's the last thing you want. You're kind enough not to say it to my face, but I guess you're too nervous to continue with our…friendship, so I'm solving the problem and getting out of your life!'

Lindy felt her throat constrict, and it was hard to get the words out. 'But this is ridiculous,' she protested. 'You can't…you can't finish our relationship just like that. What on earth makes you think I want that?'

'I can tell,' he said simply. 'Whenever I say or do something out of line, it obviously brings Jake to mind…' He paused for a second, then said rather harshly, 'I thought I'd tell you here—a long evening alone together, and I might not have had the guts to do it…'

Lindy stared at him uncomprehendingly. 'I don't know what you mean,' she whispered. 'I thought you wanted us to go on—to be in Italy together.'

Mike shook his head. 'It might, as you said, be a disaster,' he commented dryly. 'At the conference this week I had time to think about us, and I realised that perhaps I've come into your life too soon after Jake. It's unfair to ask you to forget about him so quickly— or what he did to you.'

'But, Mike,' she burst out, 'you don't understand. I've been doing some thinking, too…'

His eyes swept over her impassioned face, cheeks slightly flushed, lips parted, and a bleak expression crossed his face. 'It's for the best,' he said gently. 'Emotionally you're not yet free to love me as I love you.'

'That's not true,' she whispered, 'Believe me, it's not true.'

There was a wild burst of laughter in the room—a

hospital porter from another department had dressed up in a nurse's uniform and was pretending to do a tango.

Mike looked up at them with a wry grin. 'Time to go, I think!' He touched Lindy's cheek gently with his finger, and looked at her steadily. 'Let me know if you ever need me for anything!' Then he said softly, 'See you around, sweetheart. It's been fun!'

She thought she saw an anguished look cross his face then he turned, and was gone.

Lindy stared with a stunned expression at the door as it closed after him, completely unable to believe what Mike had just said. Surely she hadn't seemed *that* negative when he'd apologised to her? She twisted her fingers together helplessly. What could she do? She wanted him desperately, needed his love and reassurance. It couldn't be that they'd come to the end of the line. A crushing sadness squeezed her heart. It was too late, too late to call him back, although without a shadow of a doubt she loved him, body and soul!

People had begun to drift away, calling their farewells, and automatically Lindy smiled and waved and thanked them for coming. Sheila shot a sly look at her as she cleared away some of the cans.

'You and George Clooney seemed to be getting on well then.'

With an effort Lindy focussed her eyes on her friend. 'What do you mean, Sheila?'

Sheila giggled. 'You know very well! I'm talking about the gorgeous Mike Corrigan! I saw those kisses he stole!'

'Mike and I are just…good friends. Nothing more!' Lindy forced a lightness into her tone that she didn't feel.

'Oh, yeah? Why did he take the trouble to arrange

this for you, then?' Sheila's eyes twinkled. 'Say what
you like, I think our lovely doctor's about to fall for
you in a big way!'

Lindy shook her head, pulling on her coat so that
Sheila couldn't see her face. She didn't trust herself to
speak. Sheila couldn't be further from the truth, she
thought miserably.

As Lindy drove over to Apsley Grange, she went over
and over the words Mike had said to her, the horrible
finality of them. Had he *really* meant that the two of
them had no future? She shook her head helplessly as
she drove through the countryside. How stupid she'd
been, thinking every forceful statement Mike made
meant he was like Jake! Sadly she fingered the figure
of the little golden athlete now on the chain round her
neck, and reflected that she should have been more
forgiving when Mike had tried to apologise—she'd
thrown it back on his face, and as a consequence she'd
probably lost him for ever.

Somehow the happiness had gone out of the day,
and her excitement at seeing Angela again was tem-
pered by the awful thought that she and Mike were
finished.

Angela was waiting on the steps of the beautiful
manor house as Lindy drove up the drive. The whole
place looked like an advertisement for gracious living,
she thought wryly—the sweeping lawns, the mullioned
windows and the lovely mellow stonework. It seemed
incredible that she, Lindy, brought up in a relatively
poor household, should have any connection with all
of this!

She jumped out of the car, and went forward with a
bright smile on her face—no way would she allow

Angela to know about her unhappy romance. This was her birthday, and Angela was longing to enjoy it with her!

To her surprise, Angela's smile was very half-hearted. She looked exhausted and worried and, although she embraced Lindy warmly, seemed to have lost the sparkle she'd had at their first meeting.

Lindy looked at her with concern. 'Are you all right, Angela? Is anything wrong?'

Angela gave a shaky little laugh, then blew her nose, obviously trying not to cry.

'Why, Angela, something *is* wrong, isn't it? Tell me what's happened.'

'I'm so sorry, darling, to burden you with this on your birthday—I wanted it to be such a carefree evening—but it's Bernard...'

'What about him? Has he had an accident?'

Angela shook her head. 'No...no. But he's not well. I know he's not, but he utterly refuses to see anyone—says I'm fussing. When I insisted on ringing the doctor he got so worked up I gave in. The only compromise we came to is that if you thought he should see someone when you arrived, he might think about it! But it seems such an imposition when you've come to enjoy yourself.'

Lindy hugged her. 'Don't be silly! You've no idea how good it feels to be of some use to you! Let's go and see how he is—and try and talk some sense into him!'

Bernard was lying on a sofa in the beautiful drawing room, looking out over the rolling parkland. He smiled weakly at Lindy as they came in.

'Angela been telling you I'm on death's door, has

she?' he joked. 'Just got a tight chest—that's all. Nothing to worry about!'

Lindy swept an assessing eye over Bernard's face. The last time she'd seen him he'd been ruddy-complexioned, full of life. Now there was a pallor about him, a slight sheen of perspiration on his brow. She sat down beside him and smiled reassuringly. She guessed Bernard wasn't feeling as jokey as he sounded.

'You say you've got a tight chest—any pains anywhere?' she asked gently.

'A few,' he said unwillingly, glancing across at Angela rather sheepishly.

Lindy turned to Angela. 'You know what I'm dying for after work?' she said. 'A huge cup of steaming tea. You wouldn't be an angel and get me one while I talk to Bernard?'

Angela clapped her hand to her mouth. 'Of course! How selfish of me—you must be exhausted! I'll bring one in a minute!'

She whisked out, and Lindy leant forward again to Bernard. 'Now,' she said sternly, 'I want the truth while Angela's out of the room—just how ill do you feel?'

He made a face and then said in a hesitant voice, 'I just don't feel quite right—little niggling pains around my chest and shoulder, slight shortness of breath. But I didn't want to worry Angela. She was so excited about you coming here on your birthday—and so was I. And now,' he said mournfully, 'I've gone and spoiled it all anyway!'

'What absolute nonsense!' declared Lindy briskly. 'But you will spoil it if you continue to be so stubborn. I want you to get your GP now!'

He took hold of her hand. 'I'm not being fussy—

honestly—but I don't like my doctor. He's such a pompous man. I've been meaning to try and change to someone else but, being in the rudest of health normally, I never got round to it. Couldn't *you* diagnose what's wrong? I'll do what you say!'

He looked at her pleadingly and she gave a little laugh. 'Is that a promise?' she asked.

'Of course!'

'I certainly think we need a doctor or for you to go to hospital—I can tell you what I think might be wrong with you, but I'd like someone here to back me up.'

'I don't want to go to hospital,' he said gruffly. 'If you know a reputable doctor, ask him to come!'

Lindy stared at Bernard for a second. Mike's last words floated back to her—'Let me know if you need anything…'

'I think I know just the man,' she murmured. 'A very competent colleague.'

Despite his discomfort, Bernard flicked a perceptive glance at her. 'Is he your boyfriend, then?' he asked gruffly.

Lindy blushed. 'Unfortunately not,' she admitted lightly. 'I think I've blown it on that front—work and romance probably don't mix!'

Bernard grunted. 'Don't know about that,' he commented drily. 'Work was where Angela and I fell in love!'

Mike finished listening to Bernard's chest, and pushed his stethoscope back in his pocket. He grinned down at the older man.

'It sounds OK to me at the moment—but that's just a rough guess. You really do need to come to hospital and have some tests. I think, like Lindy, that you've had an angina attack—a warning perhaps that your arteries are a bit furred up.' He pointed sternly down to the box of cigars on the table beside Bernard. 'Best to throw those away from now on!'

'It's so kind of you to come all this way, Dr Corrigan,' said Angela rather tearfully. 'On a Friday night as well!'

'No problem,' he smiled, his eyes locking with Lindy's for a moment. 'I wasn't doing anything anyway! And, please, call me Mike!'

'You will stay and have dinner with us, won't you—please?'

Mike shook his head. 'That's very kind, but what Lindy and I really want is to take Bernard into hospital. I'm going to ring St Luke's now and tell A and E to expect us in half an hour.' He turned to Bernard. 'It's really for the best, you know. It could be something quite trivial, but I think you and Angela would both feel better if we knew what was happening in that chest of yours.'

Bernard heaved a deep sigh. 'Oh, all right,' he grumbled. 'If it pleases you!'

Mike and Lindy exchanged amused glances—he was doing it to make them feel better apparently!

'I'll take Bernard,' declared Mike. 'Angela, you can go with Lindy in her car. Right! I'll make that phone call now!'

Lindy laid a hand on his arm as he went out. 'Thanks, Mike,' she said softly.

As she and Angela followed Mike in his car they chatted to each other happily, as if they'd known each other for years.

'We'll have to have a proper celebration of your birthday when Bernard's sorted out,' said Angela. 'I can't tell you what a relief it was when you came. He thinks he's invincible, but he was prepared to listen to you as a professional—and because he's fallen for you in a big way!' she added smilingly.

She flicked a quick glance at Lindy's profile as she drove along. 'What a nice man this Mike Corrigan seems to be,' she said casually. 'I suppose he's married with a family?'

Lindy steered round a corner very carefully. 'No,' she replied lightly. 'He probably works too hard to bother with that sort of thing!'

Angela smiled to herself. 'Do you think so?' she murmured.

'They want to keep Bernard in,' explained Mike to Angela. 'He's had a series of tests and, whilst there's nothing major to worry about, a small irregularity has shown up. They'll do more assessments tomorrow. He's in the best place, you know,' he added kindly, looking at her worried face.

'The best thing you can do Angela, is have a very good night's sleep,' said Lindy firmly. 'Why don't you stay at my flat? I'll have the spare bed made up in a trice, and you'll be nice and near to see Bernard to-morrow.'

Angela shook her head firmly. 'That's sweet of you, but I think I'll be fine in my own bed—and I've got the dogs to think of, too.' She looked a little anxiously at them. 'You wouldn't mind taking me back to Apsley, would you? At least then I'd have my own car tomorrow.'

'Of course—if that's what you want.'

And so they drove Angela back to Apsley Grange, and suddenly Lindy realised that she would be alone in the car with Mike on the journey back to Manorfield! Her heart thumped uncomfortably against her ribs. Was this her chance to make amends, persuade him that perhaps they hadn't reached the end of their romance?

It was still light as they started back after dropping Angela home, a glorious evening with a red sky showing in the hills beyond Manorfield.

'Be a nice day tomorrow,' ventured Lindy, casting a quick look at Mike under her lashes. She watched his slim, strong hands on the steering-wheel and longed to put her own hands on top of them. 'It…it was really good of you to come out and see Bernard—it seemed the only way.'

He laughed. 'Good job I did! I've learned a lot of things tonight, one way and another!'

Lindy stared at him as the car rushed through the countryside. 'What do you mean?' she asked cautiously. She hadn't actually mentioned that Angela was her newly found mother—she'd just implied that the couple were friends of hers. Somehow it had seemed too complicated to go into over the phone when Bernard had needed attention.

He glanced back at her. 'You're a dark horse, aren't you?' he murmured. 'Bernard told me quite a few things about you when we were going to the hospital!' He looked at her sharply. 'I hope you didn't think I was prying, but Bernard was very voluble—trying to keep his mind off things, I suppose.'

Lindy looked straight ahead of her. 'So,' she said quietly, 'what did you learn?'

Mike had stopped at the set of traffic lights on the road near her flat, and didn't speak until they'd changed. 'I learned that you and I had a lot in common, for one thing!' he said at last.

'I don't understand you!' She looked at him in a puzzled way. 'I thought you were going to say you'd learned that Angela was my real mother—you did discover that, didn't you?'

Mike stopped the car outside Lindy's flat and smiled at her. 'I think we'd be more comfortable discussing these things inside your place—not in the front seat of a car—don't you?'

Lindy's blood pounded in her veins as she opened the door. Suddenly things had changed round again, and the flat, sad feeling she'd had after her surprise party had altered to a nervous excitement.

He watched as she tossed her handbag on the settee. 'Seems like a replay of another evening we had here,' he said softly. 'Only then I didn't know much about you, although I knew I liked you...very much.' He gave a low chuckle. 'I didn't realise, for instance, that you and I have already met. It was many years ago—long before I came to St Luke's!'

Lindy stared at him, her large tawny eyes baffled. 'What do you mean—we've met before?'

Mike took her arm and rolled back the sleeve, his finger tracing the raised white scar on her skin. 'You remember how you got this scar—the accident you had?'

She nodded, frowning. 'Of course I do—it was scary. I remember it very vividly.'

'Do you remember who was there at the time it happened? Somebody perhaps who saw the whole thing?'

'Yes...' she said slowly. 'Yes, there was a boy there. He had a handkerchief and pressed it to my arm. He...he was very kind to me and called for help.'

Mike smiled at her, and suddenly Lindy's eyes opened very wide and she took a deep intake of breath.

'*You?*' she whispered. 'It was you who helped me? You were at Oaklands Home, too?'

'On and off for a few years, whenever my mother couldn't cope,' he said quietly. 'You see, it was because of your accident that I decided I wanted to do medicine.' He chuckled suddenly. 'All your fault!' Then he tilted her face towards his and looked very seriously into her eyes. 'Little did I know that I'd meet you years later. Was it lucky chance or fate that brought us together?'

Lindy sat down very suddenly—it was hard to take in. Mike had been the boy who'd helped her all those years ago? She gazed up at him in amazement.

'How strange,' she breathed. 'You know, you probably saved my life! I...I have rather a lot to thank you for!'

He sat down besides her, taking her hands in his. 'There was another thing Bernard let slip,' he said softly.

'Something else?'

'He inferred that perhaps you didn't think too badly of me after all!'

She blushed. 'I only said I didn't think work and romance worked...'

He grinned slyly. 'Really? Well, after what he told me I'm prepared to give it a go!'

Lindy's pulse suddenly bounded into overdrive—and something very like happiness began to wash over her. Dare she think that this was a chance to start again? She gazed at his handsome, kind face and took a deep breath. 'I've something to say to you, Mike. I tried to tell you at the party this evening, but you got in first!'

She lifted the little gold athlete from her neck. 'I...I don't want this to be a farewell gift, Mike. I never wanted us to part, you know, and…and things have suddenly become much clearer to me now.'

'What kind of things, Lindy?'

She put up a hand and stroked his strong, tanned face. 'Well, now I know for certain that you never were, and never could be, compared to Jake Burton. I must have been completely crazy to even think it.'

His eyes twinkled at her amusedly. 'Good news indeed,' he murmured. 'How can you prove it?'

She looked at him mischievously, then drew his face towards her and kissed him hard on his lips, drawing him back on top of her as she fell back on the sofa. Mike slowly and deliberately undid her silk shirt and pulled it back from her shoulders, then he sighed, his eyes feasting on her, lingering over her full breasts and curving waist. She put her arms round his neck and pulled him down to her.

'That certainly helps to prove it,' he said huskily. 'Perhaps this is the right time to find out more about each other. I want to discuss that holiday in Italy, and how I'm going to persuade my sister that it wouldn't be a good idea to come with us…' He paused and bent down to cover her soft skin with light kisses so that she moaned softly with pleasure and hot desire.

'Mostly, however,' he continued softly, 'I want to do something I've wanted to do ever since I first saw you.' He grinned down at her. 'It would be easier to do it in the bedroom…'

The sky was peppered with stars twinkling in dark velvet, and the silver sickle of a moon hung over the little village. It was high on a hill, and the mingled smell of woodsmoke and mimosa blossom rose up to the little verandah where they stood.

'This is perfect,' breathed Lindy. She pressed her body close to Mike's, feeling his instant answering response and smiled to herself in the darkness. The past two weeks had been magical—after they had delivered Carlo Romoli safely back to his home in Rome, they had come to the Romoli holiday villa in the ancient Tuscan hills.

Mike's sister had not taken up the offer of an Italian holiday, saying she couldn't take Max out of school. Mike hadn't argued! And then how sweet it had been, reflected Lindy happily, to finally be alone together—to wander through the olive groves and vineyards during the day, stopping off for picnic lunches of rustic bread and cheese and light white wine. In the evenings they lingered over long meals before making love in the high white bedroom of the old building.

Lindy turned to Mike and pressed her face into his warm neck. 'I want to keep this moment for ever,' she whispered.

Mike smiled down at her tenderly, into her eyes the colour of beech leaves in autumn. 'We'll come back very soon,' he promised. 'Wouldn't it be a good place for our honeymoon?'

'Is that a proposal?' she asked cheekily. 'If it was, my answer's yes!'

His eyes blazing with desire he bent his mouth to her lips, plundering their soft fullness. He lifted the straps of her satin nightdress and let it fall with a slight whispering rustle to the ground. He held her back from him for a second, his gaze travelling over the whiteness of her body in the moonlit night.

'It most certainly was a proposal,' he murmured.

Then he picked her up in his arms and carried her into the high white bedroom.

MILLS & BOON®

Makes any time special™

Copyright © Harlequin Enterprises Limited 1997
All rights reserved

Mills & Boon publish 29 new titles every month. Select from...

Modern Romance™   **Tender Romance**™

Sensual Romance™

Medical Romance™ **Historical Romance**™

MAT2

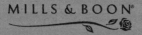

Medical Romance™

REDEEMING DR HAMMOND *by Meredith Webber*

Busy obstetrician Mitch Hammond was in desperate
need of some order in his life. Beautiful and determined
Riley Dennison agreed—Mitch needed redeeming—but
now she had to convince him that she would be perfect
as his bride!

AN ANGEL IN HIS ARMS *by Jennifer Taylor*

After the trauma in Dr Matthew Dempster's past he'd
shut everything else out, not wanting to love and lose
again. But could paramedic Sharon Lennard persuade
Matthew to let her into his life and together find the
love they both richly deserved?

THE PARAMEDIC'S SECRET *by Lilian Darcy*

When a powerful attraction flows between Anna
Brewster and her new air ambulance colleague Finn
McConnell, she knows she's in for trouble—especially
as it seems Anna's cousin is expecting his baby.
Somehow she has to resist...

On sale 6th July 2001

*Available at most branches of WH Smith, Tesco,
Martins, Borders, Easons, Sainsbury, Woolworth
and most good paperback bookshops*

0601/03a

MILLS & BOON®

Medical Romance™

THE CONSULTANT'S CONFLICT by Lucy Clark

Book one of the McElroys trilogy

Orthopaedic surgeon Jed McElroy refused to see past Dr Sally Bransford's privileged background and acknowledge her merits. He fought his attraction to her, but as they worked side by side, the prospect of making her a McElroy was becoming irresistible!

THE PREGNANT DOCTOR by Margaret Barker

Highdale Practice

Dr Adam Young had supported GP Patricia Drayton at the birth of her daughter, even though they'd just met! Reunited six months later, attraction flares into passion. Her independence is everything, but the offer of love and a father for Emma seems tantalisingly close…

THE OUTBACK NURSE by Carol Marinelli

In isolated Kirrijong, Sister Olivia Morrell had her wish of getting away from it all, and Dr Jake Clemson suspected that she had come to the outback to get over a broken heart. If she had to learn that not all men were unreliable, could he be the one to teach her?

On sale 6th July 2001

Available at most branches of WH Smith, Tesco, Martins, Borders, Easons, Sainsbury, Woolworth and most good paperback bookshops

0601/03b

 MILLS & BOON®   S&S/RTL4

MIRANDA LEE

Secrets & Sins

Passion, sensuality and scandal
set amongst Australia's rich and famous

A compelling six-part linked family saga.

Book 4 - Fantasies & The Future

Available from 6th July

Available at branches of WH Smith, Tesco,
Martins, RS McCall, Forbuoys, Borders, Easons,
Volume One/James Thin and most good paperback bookshops

FREE

4 BOOKS
AND A SURPRISE GIFT!

We would like to take this opportunity to thank you for reading this Mills & Boon® book by offering you the chance to take FOUR more specially selected titles from the Medical Romance™ series absolutely FREE! We're also making this offer to introduce you to the benefits of the Reader Service™ —

- ★ FREE home delivery
- ★ FREE monthly Newsletter
- ★ FREE gifts and competitions
- ★ Exclusive Reader Service discounts
- ★ Books available before they're in the shops

Accepting these FREE books and gift places you under no obligation to buy; you may cancel at any time, even after receiving your free shipment. Simply complete your details below and return the entire page to the address below. **You don't even need a stamp!**

YES! Please send me 4 free Medical Romance books and a surprise gift. I understand that unless you hear from me, I will receive 6 superb new titles every month for just £2.49 each, postage and packing free. I am under no obligation to purchase any books and may cancel my subscription at any time. The free books and gift will be mine to keep in any case.

MIZEC

Ms/Mrs/Miss/Mr ....Initials ....
BLOCK CAPITALS PLEASE

Surname ....

Address ....

....

....Postcode ....

Send this whole page to:
UK: FREEPOST CN81, Croydon, CR9 3WZ
EIRE: PO Box 4546, Kilcock, County Kildare (stamp required)

Offer valid in UK and Eire only and not available to current Reader Service subscribers to this series. We reserve the right to refuse an application and applicants must be aged 18 years or over. Only one application per household. Terms and prices subject to change without notice. Offer expires 31st December 2001. As a result of this application, you may receive further offers from Harlequin Mills & Boon Limited and other carefully selected companies. If you would prefer not to share in this opportunity please write to The Data Manager at the address above.

Mills & Boon® is a registered trademark owned by Harlequin Mills & Boon Limited.
Medical Romance™ is being used as a trademark.